JANE DOE SCARLETT

BY KRIS CALVERT

Cover by jim@insigniadesign.com
Edited by Meg Weglarz and Molly J. Kimbrell

ISBN: 978-1-943180-23-3

Calvert Communications, Lexington, KY 40515

Acknowledgements

Many thanks to **Heather** for being my thriller and suspense partner in crime. I wouldn't want to shoot pretend bad guys and sit through police procedural classes with anyone else.

Thank you to **Jim**, my friend and colleague for over twenty-five years. You are by far the best designer in the world. I'm so privileged to know you and am thankful for you every day.

Thank you to **Meg and Molly** my editing ninjas. Molly, what would I do without text to grammar advice?

Finally, thank you to my adoring husband, **Rob** who literally had to hold my hand through most of this year and cheered me on during this three book series. And to my two children who aren't children anymore, **Luke** and **Haley** who always find time to ask about what I'm writing about in the middle of their own busy lives. I love you all, with all my heart.

Other Books by Kris Calvert

Jane Doe – Scarlett
Jane Doe 2 – Alice
Jane Doe 3 – Catherine

Sex, Lies & Sweet Tea – Book One
Sex, Lies & Lipstick – Book Two
Sex, Lies & Pearls – Book Three
Sex, Lies & Lace – Book Four
Sex, Lies & Bourbon – Book Five
Sex, Lies & Black Tie – Book Six
Sex, Lies & Diamonds – Book Seven – 2018
Sex, Lies & Champagne – Book Eight – 2018
Sex, Lies & Leather – Book Nine – 2018

Beauty

Lead Me From Temptation
Deliver Me From Evil – 2018

Be Mine – a Valentine's Day Novella
Sparks Fly – an Independence Day Novella
Roses are Wrong, Violet's Taboo

Kris Calvert's Website:
www.kriscalvert.com

For Luke

"Hardships make or break people."
—Margaret Mitchell, *Gone With the Wind*

DAY TWENTY-TWO | 0400 HOURS

S HE BLEW AT the stray hair stuck to her lip with a puff of exasperation and eyed the corndog turning on a greasy roller at the cut-rate gas station. The meat products looked questionable. The store smelled of motor oil and mop water. She took short breaths to keep from inhaling the stench. Her stomach rumbled with a gurgled sigh. She'd been tracking nonstop for forty-eight hours which meant two things: she was hungry and her target was dead.

She fingered the plastic cap of the used syringe tucked deep in the pocket of her grey zip-up hoodie. It needed to go. So did she.

"Yeah?" The clerk asked. He barely glanced her way. There was no need to. She was as average as a woman could be—not too tall or short, not too large or small. Her hair wasn't blonde, it wasn't brown. She was neither beautiful nor homely. She was everyone and no one at all. "Can I help you?" The fleshy, unshaven man's scowl spoke volumes of unhappiness over his quiet tone and stained wife-beater. She sized him up from head to toe. Autopilot. *Always prepared. Always alert.* She took in every detail of the lone cashier and her surroundings. The front door was five paces left, the gun under the counter, one.

"Key to the bathroom." She made the request with no inflection in her voice. She was calm. Quiet. Unassuming. Hungry. Her stomach groaned loud enough for the clerk to take notice. "And a corndog."

"Dollar and four cents." He placed the key on the counter with a thud. It hung from a long, squared block of wood that proclaimed the washroom rules: *no funny business, no smoking, no crack, no banging dope, no smoking meth, no sex and no sleeping.*

Digging four quarters and a nickel from the front pocket of her jeans, she placed the coins on the counter. He grumbled something under his breath. She didn't listen. She didn't care.

Slipping a thin sheet of wax paper from a cardboard box covered in mustard stains, she opened the lid to the hotdog roaster and took the last corndog from the spinning cylinder by its stick.

Exiting the double glass doors, three rusty bells jingled overhead and she took a quick left to the dented metal and weather-beaten door marked *NOmen* in black Sharpie over the female stick figure.

The key had to be jiggled. She placed the corndog in her mouth and used both hands.

Inside, the cracked florescent light flickered above, illuminating the dirty room that smelled of rotten eggs to a greenish glow. She rehashed the idea of taking a pee when she saw the disgusting toilet. It had been just as bad in the Men's Room.

Taking the syringe from her pocket, she cracked her stiff neck left and right. Her target had gained weight while she cased him and planned his demise. The job had gone on longer than she'd planned, and eliminating him had turned into a bigger job—literally.

She'd killed him on an equally nasty toilet next door, watching the life drain from his face without contrition. His bathroom key had the same rules as hers with the exception of sleeping. Apparently the men were allowed to nap at the Circle M Quick Stop on the outskirts of Dallas. The women, not so much.

A quick and lethal dose of succinylcholine or *sux* to the back of the shoulder after following him into the crapper was the beginning of his end. She'd managed to drop his pants to his ankles and rest his lifeless body on the dirty commode before he drew his final breath. It was over quickly as it should've been, the entire scenario unfolding in less than a minute. The planning had taken longer. Twenty-two days to be exact.

Carefully cased, she knew her target frequented the location to conduct simple drug deals for the same reason she chose it to be his deathbed—anonymity. The gas station and convenience store had no security system in place to document her presence, only large mirrors and fake cameras in the corners of the store to deter shoplifters. The Circle M employed a long-held belief and tradition in Texas—God and guns. If you were a thief, you'd meet both. Hence, the only security on the property was a sawed-off shotgun under the counter and employees who appreciated judicious marksmanship.

She stretched her shoulders, shrugging off the tension in her tight body. Her target was dead, but in the process, she'd wrenched her neck. Now she'd suffer the consequences all because a suicide bomber who wanted to kill hundreds at the oldest rodeo in the country couldn't lay off the burritos.

Snapping the cap and needle to the syringe, she tossed it into the toilet and kick-flushed with her boot before peering into the trashcan in the corner. A similarly wrecked needle sat atop the pile of paper towels and rubbish, evidence that a heartbroken junkie would need to find a new way to get high.

Using the last scraps of toilet paper to shield her hand, she unlocked the door and turned the handle—the corn dog still resting between her lips.

Placing the wooden block with the bathroom rules under her armpit, she pulled a small plastic bottle of hand sanitizer from the back pocket of her jeans, squirting a glob into her palm. The smell of rubbing alcohol filled her nose and she took a deep breath before biting off the end of the corn dog she'd waited so patiently to eat.

Backing into the store butt first, she leaned over the counter allowing the key to drop from under her wing with a clank.

The attendant looked her way for the first time. She didn't make eye contact and backed out the same way she came in. She'd walk the two miles to a furnished apartment to gather the backpack by the door which contained a change of clothes, an ancient iPod filled with opera music, cash, essential supplies, a small tin box and an overdue library book left on her doorstep two days ago concealed inside a plain brown box from her only link to each assignment, *Crow*. She didn't know the identity of her contact, whether it was a man or a woman. She didn't care. Crow watched from above. Crow gave the orders. *She* followed them.

She'd be wheels rolling on the next bus out of the dusty town before anyone would miss number *Seven* on the kill list—a man known to have masterminded two separate terrorist attacks in London and Turkey. His plans for

Texas were now merely notes and an unarmed bomb sitting quietly in the room he rented over a Tex-Mex dive. Seven was now slumped forward on the toilet seat, dead from a heart attack while burning a mule—at least that would be the official coroner's report.

Dubbing the accomplished mission as *The King*, she began her two mile walk to the ramshackle space she'd called home for twenty-two days, humming the only Elvis song she could recall, *Suspicious Minds*. She didn't look back. She never looked back.

She chewed the final bite of her corndog before slipping the empty stick into her pocket. She was an assassin, not a litterbug.

DAY ONE | 0600 HOURS

THE RIDE WAS bumpy enough to make sleep difficult. She'd scored a seat alone in the middle of the bus where she was close to the bathroom, but also near her evacuation point—the front door. A middle-aged man with a smoker's cough and a bag of peanuts introduced himself as Marvin when he'd boarded six hours ago. Marvin had refused to stop eating even though he choked on his peanuts every two minutes, hacking up a lung and spreading whatever virus lurked in his sputum to everyone around him.

She slid deeper into her seat, wrapping her scarf over her nose and mouth. The smell of Typhoid Marvin's peanuts was everywhere and the nutty odor took her back to a place in her mind she visited only occasionally, and to a boy. Jack. For the first time in weeks, the corners of her mouth curled into a grin.

Jack Blue, with his long hair and scarred hands that were usually covered in pencil lead from sketching something inappropriate—like a penis with a fedora. His drawings were a surefire way to upset their God-fearing foster mother, Carol. Her smile widened at the thought of the woman's appalled face. Jack always joked they were like the *Brady Bunch*, but there were only four foster kids in the house at the time. Jack, whose real mother burned his hands to a crisp on the stovetop when he was three because he wouldn't stop crying. Maggie, who was a crack baby and struggled both emotionally and in school. Ernest, whose mom was a hooker and drug addict, but constantly tried to regain custody when she really didn't want it. And the girl without a name, family or past. Jane. Jane Doe.

Jack loved peanut butter more than any person Jane had ever been around—maybe even the peanut butter eating sonofabitch General Richard Painswick—her commanding officer while deployed. Both Jack and *Bring the Pain*-swick ate it on everything and *with* everything. In the beginning, Jane thought it was weird, but soon realized everyone was a little weird.

Jack once told Jane the only thing kids like the two of them could do for each other was to *be there*. Surprisingly enough it was similar to what Painswick taught; have your fellow Marine's *six*. Jack and Jane were abused kids in foster care. Jane could only imagine what Painswick had seen in his forty-five years in the Marine Corps.

Jack was the only kid in foster home number six Jane trusted. She'd not seen or spoken to him in fifteen years, but she kept up with him via social media. Jane had fake accounts. It was part of the communication network set up for her when she took her position. Still, she wasn't Jack's friend—she wasn't anyone's friend, but his accounts weren't private so at the very least she was able to see the photos of him at art school, with his girlfriend and eventually, with his new baby girl.

"Peanut?"

The raspy voice took her out of her own head. She stared through Marvin, her eyes piercing into the man's insecurities. He backed down. "Guess not."

Turning away from the group of misfits and miscreants loaded on the bus, she stared out the window, listening to the tiny voice of a baby girl sitting with her mother one row in front of her. The temperature had dropped, and a magical fog rolled through the woods and along the highway. Her twenty-three-hour trip was half over. Jane was anxious to transfer to a new bus in less than ten minutes in New Orleans where she hoped Marvin would be going in another direction.

Jane pulled the dog-eared paperback from under her hip and opened it again to where she'd left off. To anyone watching, she was poring over *Gone with the Wind.* For Jane, it was the details of her newest assignment.

An old, hand-stamped library card in the back of the book revealed a series of numbers which looked like due dates or official library catalogue information. To Jane they were an Ottendorf Cipher. Page numbers, lines on that page and a numbered word in the line of text. The book was one of the only possessions she'd kept from her serviceable apartment in Texas. She'd either burned or trashed everything she'd touched, tossing any leftover evidence into a dumpster behind a diner across town. The towels and bed linens she'd used were shoved into a Goodwill drop box. She took only what she needed to make it to her next destination. Atlanta, Georgia.

The information on the card was already stored in her mind—a place where numbers and words could be recalled with remarkable precision. A photographic, or eidetic memory was what it had been referred to when she was in the Marines. For Jane, it was how she was wired. Words and numbers. If she saw them or read them, she knew them.

    565 17 11 KILL
    1128 16 7 SOLDIER
    763 3 5 ATLANTA
    197 7 5 GEORGIA
    499 16 5/6 FIVE POINTS
    327 19 3 WAREHOUSE
    327 16 12 MILLION
    [13]
    33.7657 84.3494

Her mission was to kill a known terrorist and soldier of the caliphate. Number Thirteen. She knew his name. She knew all the names on

The List but never used them. She refused to honor any of them by saying their name—ever. In the past year and a half, she'd disposed of five numbers. They were everything from jihadists to an ugly ball-sack of a redneck asshole—number Twenty-six. A white supremacist that headed up a neo-Nazi organization, he had plenty of C-4 and a plan to bomb an African-American church in Little Rock, Arkansas. Twenty-six was Jane's only kill with a weapon. She'd done away with him using his own gun, making it look like a cross between suicide and a Darwin Award. Yes, he'd shot himself, but the death scene could've easily been interpreted as if he'd not checked the chamber of his old-ass muzzle-loader before deciding to clean it. Just before she pulled the trigger with his finger, she stared into his hatred-filled eyes and tattooed face. Then whispering with a smile and her best hillbilly accent she said, *'watch 'is.'*

Her instructions for each target were clear—at least to her. She'd find her latest kill mission, number Thirteen, in or around an Atlanta, Georgia warehouse in the Five Points area of town with the coordinates 33.7657

84.3494. Her compensation wasn't the usual five hundred thousand, but a cool one million dollars.

Jane didn't care about the money. Not really. She knew someday she'd walk away and never look back. She would have to. Eventually she too would have a target painted on her, just like her kill assignments. It could happen after a change in the American political regime, or when the funding dried up. Whatever the reason, Jane was certain there would be a cleanup and the agents who'd served their country like her would be eliminated. Literally. Jane had an end target, and when that kill mission was accomplished, she would leave everything behind, ignoring any attempts to be pulled back. Until then, she was naked. If she was caught or implicated in a death in any way, she would be disavowed. The Coywolf Project existed only in the minds of a few—and those people could be counted on one hand. She was a stealth operative, part of a highly mobile tactical assault team. A deep cover agent. The Coywolf name, like the project, was a hybrid. Because coyotes disliked hunting in forests and wolves preferred it, the domesticated part of the hybrid—the dog—made the coywolf tolerant of people and noise—friendlier than the true killer they were. Somehow Washington found the comparison fitting. Jane didn't care what they called it. The mission remained the same: track and eliminate known terrorists on domestic soil without ceremony or evidence. She worked *off the books*. No files. No notes. No evidence. Her orders came from the highest office of the United States. And she always followed them. *Always*.

Jane possessed a fertile imagination and a penchant for executing improvised, but brilliant, plans. An operative with impeccable physicality, her mental health report teetered somewhere between fearless and psychotic. With an impressive number of kills to her record, she'd cheated death more times than she cared to count. Jane Doe was quite simply a killing machine with ice running through her veins. Still, Jane's finest attribute was her patience. Because of that, she was willing to wait until a particular number came up before retiring for good. The number belonging to one man and the very reason she agreed to sign on with the project.

She'd play along, terminating the kill assignments sent to her, but continued hoping and even praying for an assignment to end the life of one known terrorist in particular. Number Three. Siad al Daleel ul Khyayraat—The Instructor, or SDK. A man so heinous and dangerous he'd been in hiding since the Taliban was overthrown in Afghanistan. That didn't stop him from issuing orders from whatever cave he was living in.

Three was a mastermind. An American citizen born to wealthy foreign parents studying in the States. He went home to Saudi Arabia with Mom and Dad at the age of ten, and returned to the U.S. for college. He was brilliant. He was charming. He was, for all intents and purposes, American. And he was diabolical. A senior recruiter and motivator, his fingerprints were on every major terrorist attack over the last ten years. He looked American, spoke perfect English and fit into even the most square of Midwestern societies without standing out. He held many identities to travel about the globe and he used them wisely, coming and going only when it was warranted.

The latest intel Jane had seen told her he

was Syria or Pakistan, but he would return to America. He always did. Jane would be waiting for him.

She stared at the book. Her current target, *Thirteen*, was the only number not part of the code. It was always displayed in brackets. Known for masterminding more than one embassy bombing, he was highly sought by counterterrorism agencies the world over. The million-dollar reward meant Washington was surprised to find him on American soil. Jane knew better. Creeps like Thirteen had everything they needed to move about freely—fake passports from countries not on watch lists—and money.

"Good book?" Marvin wouldn't give up.

Jane said nothing.

"Bitch," he mumbled under his breath.

Jane didn't look at him. She didn't care. She had eight more hours before she could do what she did best—be alone.

"Hi."

The tiny voice rang out between the seats and Jane pulled her eyes from the page to find a small hand reaching through the crack. It was a nice break from the creep across the aisle.

"Hello."

"I'm sorry," her young mother said leaning around the seat. "Mary Beth, don't bother the nice lady."

Jane found an honest smile. "It's no bother." The young mother wore an overly laundered, pale blue shirt with a blood stain at the collar she couldn't wash away. She was visibly overwrought. The scratches and bruises on her arms told Jane a familiar tale—abuse.

A burly, bearded man in a grey t-shirt and dirty jeans sat in a huff next to the young mother. The acrid stench of the chemical toilet he'd just befouled accompanied him.

Jane sat back in her seat and opened the book to the back flap of the paperback. Inside was a quote from Margaret Mitchell.

If the novel has a theme it is that of survival. What makes some people come through catastrophes and others, apparently just as able, strong and brave go under? It happens in every upheaval. Some people survive; others don't. What qualities are in those who fight their way through triumphantly that are lacking in those that go under? I only know that survivors used to call that quality, 'gumption'. So I wrote about people who had gumption and people who didn't.

Jane rolled the word over in her head. *Gumption.* Scarlett—a woman who was able to walk out of catastrophe a survivor. It reminded her of the advice given by her favorite teacher when Jane discovered she didn't have a financial path to college after aging out of foster care. *Always make sure the fire inside you burns hotter than the fire around you, Jane.*

"What the fuck you think you doin', bitch?"

The hair on the back of Jane's neck stood on end and she focused her attention on the couple's reflection in her window.

"I'm sorry." The young mother cowered then covered the child's head with her hand, shielding her from the vitriolic rage spewing from her partner's mouth. The toddler picked up on her mother's angst and immediately began to whimper. It was a sound Jane knew well. It was more than fear. It was cultivated despair. Even at her young age, the child knew what was to come.

"I swear woman. You piss me off to no end. Shut that baby the fuck up. You know I can't take her cryin' like that."

They were nearly to the New Orleans bus station when the asshole stood to search for something in the storage bin overhead. Jane joined him, lurching into his body when the bus took a wide turn.

Pinching was an art she'd learned from other foster kids and with the skilled hands of a pickpocket, Jane pulled a wallet from the sagging ass-end of the man's jeans then sat at once, half-heartedly apologizing.

He shot her a dirty look and sat as the child's whimper turned into an imploring cry. "Shut her the fuck up, I said."

"Tommy," the mother pleaded, bringing her voice down. "I'm trying. Can't you see I'm trying? C'mon Mary Beth. C'mon sweetheart. Shhhhhh."

Jane rifled through the man's wallet. There wasn't much money, probably part of his problem. His driver's license read, Thomas Kain. She memorized his address in New Orleans then closed the wallet and tucked it under her leg.

"Jesus Christ. *Shut up.*" Tommy Kain ground the words out and Jane watched him through the crack between the seats as he grabbed Mary Beth by the arm, squeezing it tight. The toddler wailed in pain. Jane white-knuckled, gripping the armrest of her seat.

The bus let out a groan as it turned into the main lot. The driver joined the twenty or so busses already at the station, lined up like crayons in a box. They pulled under the blue awning, the brakes letting out a squeal before the bus finally stopped. Kain let go of the child to gather his belongings. Jane watched him with unblinking focus and did the same.

The group began to shuffle down the aisle, anxious to get off the smelly bus. Jane kept her eyes on Mary Beth. The child buried her face in her mother's chest, looking up only once. Jane stared into her weepy eyes. Tears and snot covered the little girl's rosy cheeks and lips.

On the pavement, the smell of diesel fuel and exhaust filled the air. The bus driver pulled luggage from under the bus, throwing it on the asphalt, devil-may-care. Everyone waited for their bag—including Tommy Kain.

The young mother stepped away to the nearby sidewalk, rocking Mary Beth on her hip to console the frightened child. When Tommy picked up his duffle and slung it over his shoulder, Jane cornered him as the other passengers hustled off to their next destination.

"Did you lose this?" Jane held the wallet in the air for him to see.

He closed in. "Fuck yeah. Where'd you find that?"

The moment Kain was within reach, Jane grabbed him by the balls and squeezed, using the Marine grip she reserved for choking out the enemy. "I know who you are, Thomas Kain, 333 St. Claude Avenue." She whispered in his ear and gave his testicles a biting twist.

Kain winced in pain, but didn't speak—his breath and thoughts focused between his legs.

"If you ever, and I mean *ever*, lay a hand on that child or her mother again, I'll *find* you and I'll *end* you. I'd bet my life you've got a rap sheet longer than this pencil you call a dick." Jane's vise grip clamped down again, her hand rotating an agonizing forty-five degrees tighter.

"Fuck you." He blenched as the whispered words left his lips. Beads of sweat appeared on his forehead and his eyes began to roll back into their sockets. His vasovagal response was kicking in. His blood pressure was dropping. If she held on much longer, the white flashes dancing in his peripheral vision would take him over completely. Lights out.

"Now that we understand each other, know this: I kill people for a living, *Tommy*. I could slide the knife hidden in my boot through your ribcage, popping your heart like a water balloon and still sleep like a baby tonight. I'd end you just for shits and giggles. Now go apologize, and don't forget what we've discussed here. Do we understand each other? Say yes."

Thomas Kain's face was white, the blood all rushing to more important parts of his body. Still he managed two words. "Fuck you."

Jane released her grip only to give him a slow but still violent punch to the junk. "That's not the answer, Tommy."

"Yes," he hissed.

"Tommy?" The young mother called over the crowd as she searched for her asshole of a partner. His knees buckled and Jane released him to fall in pain to the ground. He wheezed, and cradled his manhood, spittle falling from his smarmy beard. Jane knew he was the kind of selfish shithead who gave more tender loving care to his dick than his family. In that moment, he proved it.

Jane walked to the mother and stared her in the face. "*You* are in control of your life. If you want to leave, *leave*. Understand?"

The young woman nodded.

"Repeat after me," said Jane. "Eight hundred, seven nine nine, safe."

The young mother looked over Jane's shoulder at Tommy Kain, now on all fours, puking in the bus lot.

"*Say it.*"

"Eight hundred," she replied, finally looking Jane in the eye. "Seven nine nine, safe."

Jane threw her backpack over her shoulder and walked away. She didn't look back. She never looked back.

DAY TWO | 1300 HOURS

THE APARTMENT COMPLEX looked more like on old motel than the three story walk up it was. Shaped like a horseshoe, there were a total of thirty apartments and a parking lot big enough for half of them. It wasn't anything special. White stucco blocks that were green from moss and water runoff, it had iron stairs and railings painted black. It wasn't ideal. It didn't matter.

Jane figured the gangly manager to be the son of someone in charge—too young to be the owner, too old to want a career managing a low-rent apartment complex in a less than desirable part of Atlanta.

"Here we go," he said opening the door.

The apartment smelled of fresh paint and cleaning solution.

"It's pretty quiet around here, Miss

ah…Miss?"

"Scarlett." Jane said the word without looking at him. There was no need. She already knew his name—Jeb—from the business card he'd shoved in her hand when she walked into the leasing office.

"That's a right pretty name, you know we love our Scarletts here in the South. She's a hero—"

"Yeah, I get it." Jane took a look through each window, her hands shoved deep in her pockets. Every location, every space she occupied, she had an evacuation plan. This apartment would be no different than the others she'd lived in for the past year and a half.

Jane was polite. Jane was professional. But Jane had an eye to abandon any location and a plan to kill everyone she met. To Jane, there were three kinds of people: Distractions, which she would tolerate. Problems, which she'd deal with. And targets, which she'd eliminate. Jeb was a distraction and his sheepish manner annoyed Jane.

"Anyway. We mostly have seniors, some singles—you know, men going through divorces. And a few…ah…families."

Jane turned around and walked into the kitchen. She opened the empty but working olive green refrigerator and ducked inside for a sniff. She didn't care the apartment was old. Dirty was a deal breaker. The only thing she remembered about foster home number four was the trash and the rats. She'd been trying to forget them both ever since.

"Families?" Jane asked.

"Ah, yeah. We have a few families here."

"You're allowing undocumented immigrants to live in your apartments." It wasn't a question. It was a statement of fact. She'd seen the family on the first floor eyeing her with obvious suspicion. People that observant had something to hide or someone to fear.

"Hmmm..." he hesitated and his face flushed with anxiety. "I don't know—I mean, I can't discuss the other tenants with you...ah Miss ah...is that going to be a problem?"

Jane scoffed. She didn't care. People who didn't want to draw attention to themselves didn't call in suspicious activity. Her arrival and departure might not go unnoticed, but it would go unreported.

Jane pulled six one hundred dollar bills

from her pocket and silently counted them off one by one. Each assignment came with instructions, supplies she couldn't get on her own, and two thousand dollars in cash for anything she might need to purchase. Jane could survive on very little and had pocketed most everything she'd been given. "Three hundred a month?"

"Yeah, but I only need the first month and a fifty-dollar security deposit. And you *don't* have to pay me in cash."

She moved in close enough to make Jeb uncomfortable, and stared only at his dirty work boots, observing that his pulse had quickened and his breathing had become shallow. He licked his mouth in a nervous rhythm, running his tongue back and forth across his bottom lip. "C'mon, *Jeb*," Jane whispered. "You and I both know you're going to pocket this cash without reporting it, so let's do each other a favor. Take the money. Give me the keys and I won't turn you into Immigration and Customs Enforcement for harboring illegals on your property, which in turn, would trigger an IRS investigation of the lovely, but far from up to building code, Beverly Court Apartments."

Jeb took the cash from her grip and placed the keys on the yellowing Formica dinette table. "Laundry room is in the basement." He shut the door without a goodbye.

Two steps behind him, Jane locked the deadbolt. She pulled a flat metal sheet from her backpack and wedged it under the door, pushing the metal plates to rest against the frame. It was just one of many gadgets she'd fabricated on her own. She'd employ a keener security system when night fell.

Jane sat on the orange and brown plaid couch and wondered how many dust mites were living in the old furniture. She'd need to shop, but for now, she needed to sleep. Lugging the Coyote Brown backpack into the bedroom, she eyed the small double bed. She'd seen worse. She'd slept on worse.

The bare mattress was free of stains, which was a plus. A mattress cover before sheets and a new comforter would give her peace of mind enough to sleep tomorrow. For now, she needed a nap.

Throwing herself on the mattress, she used her backpack as a pillow. Sleep didn't come easy so when she felt the urge to close her eyes, Jane obeyed. A couple of deep breaths in, the tension in her body eased, but not before slipping a locked and loaded gun from her bag to lay beside her head. A bird chirped outside the window and Jane stared at the ill-fitting air conditioner jammed into the window. Wadded up newspaper had been used to fill the open gaps. It kicked on with a loud hum. She closed her eyes.

"WHAT DO YOU mean you don't know?" The only case worker Jane ever had, Havis Mansoor, was assigned to her when she was found—before Jane knew what an orphan or a foster kid was. Before she realized how different she was. Now Havis had retired, leaving thirteen-year-old Jane to discuss life's most intimate details with someone she'd never met—Jennifer Mora.

"Look Jane, I realize this is a shock, but Ms. Mansoor had some issues that forced her to retire and unfortunately, without the opportunity to discuss it with you. I don't know what the issues were *specifically*, but right now we need to focus on you and your needs. Okay?"

"No. It's not okay."

"Well, I'm afraid it's going to have to be, Jane."

"This is shitty." Jane slumped into the cracked vinyl chair. It was one of the many pieces of old furniture littered about the offices of the Allegheny County Children, Youth and Families. The furniture was indicative of the agency—CYF was a place where things that others didn't want were ultimately gathered—whether it be furniture or kids.

"Please don't use that kind of language, Jane. Look," she said, leaving the confines of her desk to sit in the chair beside her. "I realize this is hard. You've only known Havis and—" she paused, sliding Jane's file across her desk to read a Post-it note stuck to the top. "Father Doheny. And now you have to talk to me. But I promise Jane, I understand and I'm going to do everything I can to make this work." Jennifer Mora pointed her finger between the two of them. "Me and you."

"I think it's hilarious when people like you tell me they understand. What is it you think you *understand* Mrs..... Mora," Jane said checking the name plate on the desk to get it right. "Were *you* left inside a dumpster like trash when you were born?"

Jennifer Mora stared into the eyes of the young teen.

Jane narrowed her gaze. "No? Have *you* lived in seven different foster homes? You know, where it starts off okay, but turns into an overcrowded zoo because your foster parents take on more and more kids for the money, *Mrs. Mora?*"

"It's *Doctor* Mora and, no."

"Have you had to fight off your foster dad *and* his sixteen-year-old son in the same week? You know, to keep them from touching you in places I'd have to show you on the *doll, Doctor* Mora? Or slept in a doghouse because you were chained there for breaking a dish in the kitchen?"

"I've read through your case thoroughly, Jane and I've done extensive research and studies with kids like you."

"Like me?"

"Yes."

"Please, enlighten me on your *knowledge* of kids like me."

Dr. Mora was steadfast in her posture and stare. It was obvious she refused to back down from the sullen adolescent. "Your test scores in school are off the charts, Jane, and yet you have lower than average grades—Cs at best. You don't cause trouble in class, but your teachers say you don't participate either."

"Haven't you heard? I'm a problem child. A troubled youth."

"Jane, I think you're bored. I think you're as smart as they come. I also think you might have an incredibly bright future ahead of you and I know I can help you navigate *it* and the next five years of your life. After you turn eighteen and graduate high school you can be on your own."

Jane leaned her tall and gangling frame forward, pushing the mousy brown hair from her blue eyes. She bit her lip and held in the urge to cry. Tears wouldn't do any good. They never had. "You mean when I *age out*. Lady, I've been on my own my *whole* life. I was *abandoned*. You can't be any more *on your own* than that."

Dr. Mora stood and walked back to her desk, but didn't sit. Instead she leaned against the wall, her hands behind her body. Jane thought it was a look of surrender—she'd seen it a lot in her years in foster care. It was easier to walk away from a kid than it was to face their issues head on. "What do you think about science, Jane?"

Jane frowned and shrugged her shoulders, rolling her eyes back in her head. "I dunno. Why?"

"All your test scores are high, Jane. But your math and science scores are exceptional." Dr. Mora began to pace inside her small office. It made Jane feel restless.

"So?"

"So, I happen to know a wonderful man who runs the engineering magnet program at Taylor Allderdice High School."

Jane shrugged. She did love math and science. They were her favorite subjects because there were questions and definitive answers. Too many other subjects were just that, *subjective.* "I can't go to school there. It's not my district. At least not right now. I mean who knows where I'll end up by the time I'm in high school?"

Dr. Mora took her seat again, a smile plastered across her face. "That's the wonderful thing about a Magnet school—once you're accepted, it doesn't matter where you live in Allegheny County. You could move a hundred times and stay at the same school."

Jane lifted her face to stare at Dr. Mora. "What do you mean?"

"Exactly what I'm saying. You stay the course with your test scores and bring your grades up and I can almost guarantee you a spot in the Engineering School. You could get some college credits while you're there." Dr. Mora sat back in her chair and crossed her arms. She was openly satisfied with herself.

"How could you ever guarantee a spot for someone like me?" Jane asked.

Dr. Mora looked away and then back to Jane. "The head of the program just happens to be a very handsome man who sleeps in the same bed as I do."

"What?"

"It's my husband, Jane."

"Oh." Jane's face blushed and she could feel the blood coursing through her body with each tick of her heart. It sounded too wonderful to be true and things that sounded too wonderful always were—at least for Jane.

"Is it a deal?" Dr. Mora asked.

"Is what a deal?"

"Bring your grades up to reflect how smart you really are, and I'll make sure you have access to the best math and science classes Pittsburgh has to offer."

Jane shrugged her shoulders, the uncertainty in her body flooding her eyes. A single tear fell.

"Education is your ticket out of the life you don't want, Jane. Do you understand that?"

Jane winced as a knock came at Dr. Mora's door. When the pounding got louder, she finally turned to face her. "Aren't you going to get that?"

———

JANE PULLED THE loaded Colt M1911 semi-automatic pistol from her side in one fluid motion as she woke with a start, sitting straight up on the side of the bed. Three knocks came at her door.

"Hello? Is anyone home?" The voice was muffled on the other side and Jane paused to look between the musty curtain and window.

She never used peepholes.

Jane removed the jam, unlocked and cracked the door, resting her gun on the backside. "Yes?"

"There you are."

The older woman wore a threadbare nightgown and two sets of glasses on her face, one stacked perfectly on top of the other like pieces in a puzzle. She was clearly unarmed and obviously confused.

"What can I do for you?" Jane asked, taking a deep breath and the opportunity to completely wake up.

"I wanted to welcome you to the neighborhood. You know, us young girls need to stick together around a place like this."

Jane couldn't stop the puzzled look from creeping across her face. "Ma'am?"

"Oh…" The old woman sighed and waved Jane off as if she was being ridiculous. "You don't look a day over twenty-five. I mean, I myself am only thirty."

Jane leaned into the doorframe. "Thirty. *Really*. What's your name, darlin'?"

"I'm Melanie Munroe, but my friends call me Melly. What's your name?"

Jane hesitated. "Scarlett."

The old woman let out a gasp, placing her wrinkled hand over her mouth in surprise. "It's meant to be. Scarlett and Melly back together again."

Jane said nothing, then softened her usual calloused edge and offered her hand. "It's nice to meet you Melanie. I don't mean to be rude, but I can't visit right now."

"Of course, of course. I understand. I'm in 3C, right up there. Third floor." The old lady pointed above her head and Jane knew Melanie Munroe would be a minor distraction. They were *on* the third floor. The woman was as confused as a little old lady with dementia could be. Jane gave her a nod.

"I'll just be going then," Melly said.

"Do you know how to get back to your apartment?"

The old woman giggled and began to walk away. "You're funny. See you around."

Jane watched her shuffle down the open corridor and glanced down into the parking lot. The junky cars were still in their same spots. It was business as usual at Beverly Court, home to illegals, one lost old lady, and a trained assassin.

THE BUS STOP was less than a block from her apartment, and came right on schedule. Jane sat in the front row across from a chain-smoking vet with a new mother behind her. The city bus puffed diesel fuel, leaving a trail of black smoke in its wake. Jane made a mental list of what she needed to buy. It was identical each time. One set of sheets, mattress encasement and cover, comforter, two bath towels, two washcloths, two alarm clocks, air freshener, a disposable camera, new supply of hand sanitizer, three pairs of underwear, one bra, one sports bra, three t-shirts, one pair of shorts, one pair of jeans, cheap running shoes, white socks, frozen dinners, a roll of duct tape, liquid bleach and one foot of twelve-gauge wire.

Jane also needed a volunteer job—one not too far from the only warehouse in Five Points. A place with lots of people and access to as much anonymous information possible. It was her favorite spot to hang out while casing a target and ultimately waiting for Three's number to come up   the library.

The wheels squeaked to a halt and Jane

hurried off, already climbing the steps to the Drake Public Library before the bus had a chance to leave the stop. Noting the security cameras near the doorways, she pulled the hood of her jacket over her head, hiding her face. When she was accepted as a volunteer—and she always was—hijacking the security system was the first item on her to-do list. Second was to locate the coordinates she'd been given to pinpoint the warehouse she was looking for.

The automatic doors opened with a breeze and cool air from inside the library blew across her face. It was a stark contrast to the spring warmth and pasty humidity. The perfume of books lingered in the air. It was a cross between old paper and ink and the thousands of hands that had touched the books. Jane's theory was that each person who read a book left a little piece of their soul inside the pages themselves. It was a tale an older librarian had told her once when she was just a kid checking out books at the Carnegie Library in Oakland. The dust, the paper, the ink, the hardbacks, they were all merely a conduit for the souls of all the people who'd read them and loved them. It was a tall tale but still an unmistakable scent. And one Jane loved more than almost anything. With no money or resources growing up, she learned early to utilize things she could get for free. Library books. Not only could she check out books to read, she could escape, not thinking about her own life. Sometimes she found a character that spoke to her very soul, as if the book was written just for her. Whether it was true or not, Jane felt as if the old librarian's tale was valid. She'd left a piece of herself in each and every story she'd read. The stories of others overcoming what seemed to be insurmountable obstacles kept her going when she was a child. Perhaps if the characters in the books found a better life, so could she.

So Jane came back to the library. Always the library. No matter the assignment, no matter the location. It fit her lifestyle of anonymity.

Dropping her hood, Jane walked to the overhead sign, *Information* and cased the empty room. There were two emergency doors in the back and every exit was equal distance from the center of the library. *Always prepared. Always alert.*

The young woman behind the desk was blonde with blue eyes so large she possessed a deer in the headlights look regardless of how smart she might've been. "May I help you?"

"Samuel Goodwin?"

"The director of the library?"

Jane narrowed her gaze. "Is there another Samuel Goodwin that works here?"

"No."

"I have a one-thirty appointment."

Doe Eyes blinked incessantly. "With?" She had a thick Southern drawl and a confused sense of purpose, confirming to Jane that sometimes you *could* judge a book by its cover.

Jane took a breath and held her tongue. The woman at the front desk would be a distraction. "I'm *looking* for Samuel Goodwin because I have an *appointment* with Samuel Goodwin."

She stared at Jane for only a moment then looked away. Jane wasn't to be trifled with. Those who crossed her on the wrong side of the path were sooner or later painfully aware of it. "Oh, I get it. Down the hallway. It's the last door on your right. You can't miss it. It's next to the *Ay-Vee* room. That stands for Audio Visual."

"Bless your heart." Jane walked away, scanning the space for additional exits, windows and more importantly, hidden areas—blind spots, meeting rooms and bathrooms. With confidence she knocked twice on the open door and plastered a pleasing smile across her face. "Mr. Goodwin? I'm Scarlett Jenkins. I'm here about—"

He waved her into his small office without standing. "The open position," he chimed. "C'mon in and shut the door if you don't mind."

Jane did as she was asked, taking the chair nearest the door. Goodwin's office had no other exit point and no windows. Without being prompted, she slid the fake resume across his desk, sat up straight in the chair, and waited.

"It's crazy you called this morning about a position. One of our part-time employees won the lottery two nights ago and as you can imagine, she's not coming back to work," he said reading the resume as he spoke. "It's a godsend that you called."

Jane stared at him.

Goodwin placed the paper in front of him, moving it about on his desk with his thumb and index fingers. He licked his lips. His eyes were slightly bloodshot and his beard a day old. Jane took a breath in through her nose and exhaled through her mouth. The smell of last night's scotch was beginning to seep from his pores even though he'd done his best to cover it with drug store cologne.

"You have more than enough experience."

Jane stared at him.

He licked the stubble in the corner of his mouth then folded his lips inside. He was visibly nervous. Skittish. "When can you start?"

"As soon as possible."

"Whatcha doin' right now?"

"Learning the ropes at the Drake Public Library?"

A small laugh escaped his lips. "Good one. I like you."

He stood, knocking his leg against an open drawer. Jane came to her feet, immediately catching a glimpse of the vodka bottle rattling about in the bottom of the filing cabinet along with a gay nudie magazine—*Hung*. Goodwin would be a distraction—a distraction she could manipulate for her own benefit.

"Let's start at the main desk. I'll introduce you to Joellen and she will get you set up with all the proper paperwork for the hiring process."

"There must be some misunderstanding," Jane said. "I'm not here to work. I'm here to volunteer. Part time."

"I assumed—"

"I'm a woman of independent means, Mr. Goodwin. I like the books and I like the quiet. Is that a problem?"

"Do you mind working like a paid employee for bupkis?"

Jane shook her head *no*.

"Then welcome to our library, Scarlett Jenkins."

DAY THREE | 0330 HOURS

JANE CRUMPLED IN the arms of the only man she'd ever trusted. His robe smelled of incense and candle wax. She'd waited outside in the snow until the end of communion before entering the church, still in the utility uniform she'd flown home in. But as soon as he uttered the words, *the mass is ended, go in peace*, she'd walked toward the altar, bumping shoulders with every parishioner trying to sneak out during the final hymn. He met her at the apse. "I didn't know where else to go," she whispered.

He ushered her into his office behind the south transept, hugging her under the wing of his heavy alb. "I was granted leave because she was my only real family." The words were soft from her lips as the tears she'd held back for thirty-six hours of travel were finally set free.

He placed her wilted body next to his on the leather sofa. "My door is always open. You know that."

Jane pulled her tear-stained face from the solid comfort of Father Doheny to look him in the eye. "Havis was the only person I cared about, Father. Well… you know…except for you."

"Grief is the price we pay for love, Jane."

"I've never known the love of a parent, Father—just the mothering kindness Havis showed me. Even after she'd retired, even when she was going through chemo, she never stopped checking on me. She never stopped asking me how I was. She was the only person in the world who cared enough to love me like I was her own. I mean, Dr. Mora and Mr. Warren helped me with school, but Havis—Havis was *everything* to me. She was the only person I've known my entire life. And now some shithead has taken it all away."

"What has happened is a tragedy—for Havis—for the other innocent people."

Jane had pictured Havis dying over and over in her mind on the long trip back to the States from Kandahar. She'd seen enough men and women fall to a bullet or blown to pieces while deployed. All she had to do was put the face of the woman she considered her mother on the stored visions in her own head. It played over and over, like a glitch in the videotape of her mind.

Father Doheny sandwiched her hands inside his. "We can only pray. We *must* pray for the souls of those lost and those who perpetrated the crime."

"You're kidding, right?" Jane pushed him away for the first time since rushing into his arms.

"We must pray they recognize the evil of their actions and turn to the way of peace and goodness."

"Excuse my language Father, but fuck that shit."

Jane stared into the rosy-cheeked face of the sixty-year-old priest. The blue eyes and blond hair that had always made the women of his parish wish he wasn't sworn to chastity, now giving way to grey. He was a handsome man. He was a compassionate man. So much so, Jane couldn't grasp his reasoning most of the time.

"You're grieving, Jane. I don't expect you

to be rational."

"Good, because I'm not. I want the man behind this attack *dead*, Father. I spent the last two years in and out of caves in the middle of nowhere chasing these…these *animals*. I've watched them murder in ways that are indescribable. Things I will never be able to erase from my mind. Things worse than what I grew up with. And we both know that's pretty damn bad."

"I can't imagine what you've been through, Jane. My heart goes out to you. I pray for you constantly. You are always on my mind, as are so many on this earth that suffer. God never promised life would be easy, but he promised he would never leave us. Vengeance belongs to Him. It is not a task for you."

Jane wiped the tears from her eyes and thought of Havis, now lying in the city morgue—a casualty of a terror attack at the community center where she volunteered. "It was a *retirement* party for God's sake—one of the employees," Jane said, taking a ragged breath. "Did you know that? Everyone left their desk—all two hundred of them, to say goodbye to a man who'd worked with underprivileged kids in Pittsburgh his entire life."

He nodded, closing his eyes as if he were saying a silent prayer.

"You knew her, Father. Havis was the kind of person who would've dragged herself from death's door to honor a man who'd given his life to help at-risk kids. And what did she get for it? Gunned down. And now, I'm going to gun *his* ass down."

"Jane." The calm in Father Doheny's voice did little to stop the wheels from turning in Jane's head. "The shooter was killed on the scene. He's dead."

"You don't understand, Father. They don't work alone. Someone else was the mastermind behind this. Someone planned it and gave the order. The leaders who tell the soldiers to carry out the missions sit in their little holes thinking they're insulated from the world. They promise these assholes a beautiful life on the other side—Paradise. Killing innocent people is the crowning achievement of their existence. Well…" Jane paced the office of the old church, turning on her heels like a soldier in drill formation. "I'll take care of that shit. I'll take care of that shit, right now."

Father Doheny kept his quiet demeanor in the storm that was Jane's fury. "Jane, the Bible says there is only one lawgiver and judge, He who is able to save and to destroy. Who are you to judge your neighbor?"

"God will judge my enemies, Father. *I'll* arrange the meeting."

The phone on Father Doheny's desk rang and Jane pointed to it. "Aren't you going to get that?"

———

THE BELL ON the wind up alarm clock sounded. It was four in the morning. Jane rose and stretched her body. She hadn't slept that hard in weeks—three to be exact. She dressed in shorts, t-shirt and running shoes while thoughts of Father Doheny rolled around in her head. She needed to call him—after this assignment was over. For now, a workout and long run through the Five Points area was on her agenda before the sun rose.

Her midnight shopping excursion to Walmart had proven to be fruitful. She got everything on her list, including a yellow sweater. Without delay, she'd settled into her quarters, booby-trapping the front door before hitting the rack.

Using one of her many *MacGyvered* defense mechanisms, she'd wired the door knob of her apartment and attached it to the charged flash on a disposable camera. If anyone touched the knob, they'd get the crap shocked out of them, allowing Jane a few precious moments to arm herself completely. She'd also sprinkled a thin layer of sand she'd found in the craft aisle in front of her door. It wasn't enough that someone would notice, but a footprint would be left behind.

She armed the apartment with the essentials: A Bowie knife taped under the kitchen dinette, her Colt M1911 secured behind the headboard of her bed, and its twin wedged behind the toilet tank in the bathroom.

Her new clothes were hanging in the closet and folded in the drawers. She had enough to keep her from doing laundry too often but not enough to care about leaving behind when she'd finally blow town. And she would. She always did.

Jane slipped on the fourteen dollar running

shoes and stretched a second time. She'd not slept on a decent bed in months, but it was a price she was willing to pay—at least until she found Three.

Her iPod sat by the bedside, charging. She'd bought it at a rummage sale, not for the device itself, but for the music its owner had downloaded. Mostly opera, the iPod was still registered to someone's deceased grandmother, Marcia Brown in Freeport, Maine. Jane didn't download music. She didn't download anything. Jane never left a footprint, digital or otherwise. She possessed no email or permanent address. She was officially declared Missing in Action in the hills of Iraq and was now legally deceased as far as the U.S. government was concerned. The only things Jane *did* have were a numbered Swiss Bank account and a safe deposit box. Someday when she claimed her money at the Swiss Bank Corporation in Zurich, her face, fingerprints and passports would be an identical match to those of the owner—Jennifer Dashwood.

Jennifer Dashwood was the name she'd chosen when she met with *The Cobbler*—a man capable of preparing any type of official document in the United States as well as other countries. They weren't fakes, but authentic identification. The U.S. government used The Cobbler to create paper identities or *shoes* for those they deemed in need. A passport in the name of Jennifer Dashwood and fifty thousand dollars in cash was stored in a safe, deep in the walls of the only man who knew Jane Doe was still alive, Father Doheny.

Between Father Doheny, Havis and Dr. Mora's husband, Mr. Warren, Jane grew up with an understanding of many faiths—Christianity and Islam, as well as Warren's idea that science and the belief in a higher power could not coexist.

Father Doheny, of Our Lady of the Holy Rosary in Pittsburgh, was getting on in years and if he died, Jane would have to find another cobbler to make her new shoes. Breaking into the hidden safe of a priest inside the sanctuary of the church was surely considered a felony or worse—a cardinal sin. Every day the clock ticked for Jane and every day she waited for a notice from Crow that Three would be her next kill assignment. Day number three of mission number six was no different.

She did fifty push-ups, one hundred sit ups, and fifty dips off the side of the bed. She'd learned to use whatever she had to stay in shape. She wasn't a combat Marine anymore, but she was combat-ready.

Mozart's *Zaide* rang out in her earbuds as she disconnected the camera, opened the door and placed a tiny square of paper at the foot of the doorjamb. If anyone entered her apartment, Jane would know. She took a large step over the thin layer of sand and shut the door behind her. She slipped the single key into a pocket inside her shorts and peered over the third floor railing looking for anyone or anything unusual. It was quiet. The same five cars were parked in their respective spots.

Jane knew the area well enough after her first two days to head out for a run in the dark. She'd make a complete square around the area, specifically passing the warehouse in Five Points located at 33.7657 N 84.3494 W twice. She wanted to *recon* the place and anyone who might be there.

The pavement felt like home beneath her feet. Exercise was her greatest release, physically and mentally. It kept her from punching people and allowed her to think and plan.

She was tracking the worst of the worst with Thirteen. A man with no motivation other than to fulfill what was required of him—kill the enemy. Thirteen was a murdering extremist—a member of the caliphate—the Islamic State. The distance that existed between men like him and the quarter of the world's population that was Muslim was deep and vast. Whatever these jihadis gleaned from the Qur'an to justify their atrocities Jane would never understand. Havis was nothing like them.

Thinking of her dear friend hardened her heart. In the four years since she'd been gunned down, Jane had also lost a best friend and fellow Marine. It was a burden she carried with her at all times. All of it had taught her not to feel. There was no need. There was no one to feel anything for. Jane needed to do her job, keep her eye on the end target and stay alive. Then she'd get out. She'd researched the KTH Royal Institute of Technology in Stockholm, Sweden. It was the oldest and largest international polytechnic university. Jane had put off college to enter on the GI Bill. Now she had enough money to pay her own tuition and at one of the most prestigious and expensive schools in the world. She wouldn't allow herself to go until her mission was complete—until Three was gone.

Jane's strides became longer as she turned the corner of the street. She ran harder, getting into the groove. She was a woman of medium stature, five foot seven to be exact. Because she was lean, she seemed taller. It was an illusion. With her frame and demeanor, Havis had once told her that with her girl-next-door looks, she could make money for college when she graduated by modeling. Or, she could join the Armed Forces. Jane chose the Marine Corps.

The song shifted to another Mozart opera tune—*Requiem in D Minor* and she picked up the pace. She neared the backside of the warehouse. The morning was quiet—the only movement came from the street lights changing from red to green, the countdown and caution hand reflecting on the asphalt with each tick of the timer.

The warehouse was silent and deserted as she slowed to take a better look. It was a ten thousand square foot, two story building. Facing north, it sat across the street from a pizza parlor and Greek sandwich shop. On the east side was an open field with a pair of overhead power line towers. To the west, loading docks for the warehouse and a large parking lot. Beyond that, the nearest building on the west side was a closed up dry cleaning store. The space behind it, wooded. By the light of the waning crescent moon, she could see a dirt path that ran along the south side of the building on the outskirts of the woods.

No lights were on inside the building, but Jane noticed two entrances and one exit next to the three bay loading dock—each big enough for a semi. The side of the building had no address or name, but the street number was faintly visible on the curb.

She continued with her run, taking a mental inventory of everything around her. The music changed and she picked up her pace as a black van passed her on the street and began to slow. Jane took the iPod from her hand and held it in the air, using the reflective face see the van's destination.

When it pulled into the dock area behind the building, Jane turned the corner and checked her watch to note the time. She wanted to memorize the tags on the van before it left. Instead of taking the entire block, she chose a back alley and cut through, taking her chances at being noticed in order to get a better view of the vehicle and anyone inside.

Her targets liked the cover of darkness to move around. Jane followed their schedules closely. She had to think like them—act like them. Jane, like the people she tracked, survived off the grid. Their communications were limited and only through secure channels.

Jane hustled through a smaller alley, carefully avoiding any trash cans or debris. She needed to see without being seen. Spotting the van still sitting at the loading dock, she stayed in the alley, waiting until she could come out on the other end of the street as if she'd taken the entire block.

Making the turn, Jane slowed to a halt. Panting, she bent over to brace herself against her knees and pretended to be short of breath. She lifted her head from studying the pavement and leaned backward to stretch her body. It was a Florida plate. Jane memorized it, then waited to see if anyone was coming or going from the building. She lingered only five seconds before she began her run again, noting the time once more.

Into the five a.m. sky she ran. She'd shower, eat breakfast and be at the library when it opened at eight. It was time for research and Jane knew where to start. FL W27 9HM.

DAY THREE | 0900 HOURS

"**G**OOD MORNING!" DOE Eyes called out to Jane, who in turn gave her a nod. Yesterday while meeting the staff, Jane had learned the blonde haired blue eyed girl's name was Rose Marie and not *Rosemary,* although to Jane it was hard to tell the difference through her southern drawl.

Jane hurried to the break room and stored the grey zip up hoodie she wore and her backpack in the recently assigned locker. Someone had used an old label maker and now the name *Scarlett* was embossed on a strip of red plastic. It made Jane think of foster home number nine. The mother labeled everything in the refrigerator with an old Dymo label maker—mostly to show the foster kids what they *couldn't* eat—which was pretty much everything.

Jane adjusted the light blue shirt over her shoulder. When she caught a glimpse of herself looking too soft, she snatched a hairband from her wrist with her teeth and pulled her long brown hair in to a tight ponytail in one fluid motion. She perched a pair of low-strength reading glasses on her nose. She didn't need the magnification, but the glasses helped to hide her face. She'd even purchased a chain to hang them around her neck so she wouldn't misplace them. It was part of her *pocket litter*—the little things she needed to carry with her to prove she wasn't an imposter. People who wore glasses knew how to keep track of them—it was rote. Habit. Jane always focused on specific attributes. Father Doheny once said, *the Devil is in the details*. He was right. When her targets missed small details, Jane found opportunity. Knowing how to pose as an imposter made her even more skilled at spotting one. It took one to know one.

Jane pushed the glasses up on her nose and walked behind the main counter where one of the librarians was working on the computer. She'd only roamed around the mainframe for a moment or two after getting a sign in and password yesterday. What she'd found was the login and password for her boss. When she was left alone, she'd hack the system and hijack the security cameras. It would go unnoticed for at least six weeks, and by then, Jane would be gone.

She stood quietly behind Stella, the senior librarian, and watched her without making a sound while a library patron wandered to the desk. The woman seeking help looked tired and frustrated. Jane had seen the face before during her rare trips to the grocery. Women with kids hanging on them, looking like they hadn't slept in years, but with the patience of Job. Jane didn't understand motherhood. Mostly, she thought of mothers as uncaring and egocentric. She felt *her* mother was selfish for leaving her to die in a dumpster. The foster mothers she'd had didn't do much to dispel her beliefs that most women were out for themselves. *Every* mother, foster or otherwise had made her feel worthless—like trash.

"Can you help me?" The woman let out an exasperated sigh and dropped her shoulders in surrender. "I need information on Christopher Brennan. It's for my daughter. She has a book report."

"He's Australian," Jane said.

Stella jumped in her seat before turning to give Jane a stare. "Lord 'a mercy! You scared me, Scarlett."

Stella's drawl didn't get under Jane's skin the way Rose Marie's did. Jane gave her an *I'm sorry* smile and continued. "He's a poet."

"So you know who I'm talking about?" The frazzled woman turned her undivided attention to Jane.

Jane took the glasses from her face, allowing the chain to catch them and nodded. She opened her mouth to begin an explanation of one of her favorite poets. Before she uttered a word, a voice spoke out.

"Then seek not, sweet, the if and why. I love you now until I die. For I must love because I live. And life in me, is what you give."

Jane listened to the words. The man behind them came into full view. Tall and dark, the tan lines around his eyes told her he'd been squinting in the sun. The dark color of his irises were stormy, a look she knew from others who'd witnessed tragedy in life. Dressed in khakis, a rumpled light blue button down shirt and an army green field jacket, he wore his aviator sunglasses on his head like they were made for that sole purpose.

Stella let out an audible gasp. The woman who'd come for Christopher Brennan stared slack-jawed into the man's face like she'd seen the sun. Jane wasn't as impressed.

"Do you work here?" The woman swallowed hard and asked her question in an openly hopeful tone, placing her hand on his shoulder as if to welcome him into her home for the first time.

He shook his head and looked at neither the woman nor Stella, but Jane. "I do not."

Jane stared him down and leaned into Stella's shoulder to whisper. "I have some books to put away."

"Okay dear."

Not wasting time, Jane picked up books from the counter and placed them on the cart. It was already stacked too high with titles to go back on the shelf, but Jane wasn't about to take the time to remove them. She wanted away from the stormy eyed stranger.

"May I help you, sir?" Stella asked of the handsome man.

The woman doing her daughter's home-work chimed in. "Wait, I was here first."

"Of course." Stella stumbled over herself as she stood. "Poetry is right over here, ma'am. Let me show you the way. Sir, I'll be right back." Stella paused and gave the attractive man a quirky smile. "Don't go anywhere."

Jane maneuvered the cart from behind the sorting desk, closing the simple wooden gate that served as a barrier between the librarians and patrons. She bumped into a bookstand, causing two large hardbacks to slide from the top of the cart as another tumbled from the top shelf nearby. Taking a step away, Jane caught the book falling from above with speed and accurate skill, then snagged the books from the top of the cart before they hit the floor with her free hand. Her reflexes were nothing short of spectacular.

"Wow." The man relaxed into a stance that was all too familiar to Jane—hands slung low on the pockets of his pants—hip cocked to one side. He looked like a soldier—only missing a sure grip on the assault rifle snugly molded to his body.

Jane liked it. She couldn't deny it. But for

her, men only served one purpose—sex. She always found the saying, *why buy the cow when you can get the milk for free?* amusing. Her motto was *don't take the whole pig when you only need a little piece of sausage.* And in Jane's experience, there'd been plenty of pigs willing to give up the sausage.

Still, Jane was picky and she'd kicked more than one man to the curb when they'd wanted what Jane referred to as simply *more*. It wasn't her style. She didn't believe in *more*. She didn't believe in love. Jane believed in the basics: food, water, sex and survival.

She moved the library cart forward only to watch him step squarely in her way, before issuing a warning without tone or inflection. "You really shouldn't do that."

A sly smile crept across his full and wind-burned lips. "Do what?"

Jane leaned her head to one side and raised a suspicious eyebrow. "Step in front of me. I might not be capable of stopping the cart. I'd hate to run over your pinky toe or something."

"That's kind of you."

"Not really. I don't want to write up an incident report."

His smile widened. "You caught those

books like Odell in the end zone. I'd say you can handle this cart just fine."

He stood grinning from ear to ear, nodding his head, waiting for a response. Jane didn't flinch.

"Are you going to tell me your name?"

Jane looked away and pushed the cart forward. He followed.

"Fine. I'll go first," he said stepping in front of the cart again, causing Jane to come to another abrupt halt. She said nothing, but blinked deliberately, giving him the face she used to ward off unwanted attention and conversation. It wasn't working.

"I'm Matt. Matt Matthews." Flashing his smile again, he adjusted the cross-body satchel over his shoulder and extended his hand. Jane brought her coolly assessing gaze from his face to his gesture and back again without moving a muscle.

Matt Matthews popped a single eyebrow and dropped his chin. It was clear he wasn't giving up.

With a deep breath Jane let him know his behavior was an inconvenience, but slipped her hand into his, squeezing his fingers in the vise grip that was her handshake.

"Jesus," he said when she pulled away. "That's some *hello* you've got. What are you, the arm wrestling champ of the South or something?"

"Or something." Jane pushed her cart away again.

"Wait," he said, walking after her. "You didn't tell me your name."

"That's right."

"Well if this is Southern hospitality, I might as well drag my Yankee ass back to Pittsburgh."

Jane stopped, but didn't turn around to meet his words. Instead, she pretended to search the cart for a book.

"Aha!" He was on her heels again. "*Pittsburgh*. You don't know Odell, but I bet you know Big Ben."

Turning, Jane folded her hands in front of her in a ladylike fashion. "Odell Beckham Jr. is a first round draft pick wide receiver for the New York Giants."

She turned and pushed her cart forward. "Greatest catch ever made."

"Wow," he whispered under his breath before calling after her. "What about Ben?"

Jane didn't turn around. It wasn't merited. Instead, she gave the reply over her shoulder. "Roethlisberger's the youngest Super Bowl-winning quarterback in NFL history."

"Wait! What?" He rushed in front of the cart, this time wedging his body against it. The look on Matt Matthews face was one of shock. "I'm impressed."

Jane shoved the cart forward just enough to push him away. "Don't be. I'm a Packers fan."

"Ho—hold up."

Jane gave him *the stare*—a cross between *I'm about to kick your ass* and *get the hell away from me.* Matt Matthews didn't seem to mind. When he continued with the shit-eating grin, she finally broke. "Look, is there something I can help you with? Because I'm not being paid to stand around and chat."

Matt pointed to the badge on Jane's shirt that read, *Volunteer.* "Looks like you're not being paid at all."

Jane took a moment to observe him objectively. He was fit, but not bulky. He looked like he could throw a punch, but probably never had. He was smart—as evidenced by his knowledge of poetry *and* football. He was handsome. Rugged. Almost pretty, in a Hollywood action star kind of way. Jane was sure he'd had his way with more than a handful of women. He was trouble. He was more than a distraction. Matt Matthews was becoming a problem.

After a long moment of silence that neither of them seemed to mind, Jane asked a question. "Did your parents really name you Matthew Matthews? Or did you choose that because you thought it sounded hip? Matt Matt? So nice, they named you twice?"

He laughed, releasing his neck and dropping his head, obviously enjoying the moment. When he looked at her again, she saw it. It was an attribute she'd learned to spot in her fellow Marines—an unspoken sense of worthiness that said, *I am real. I am genuine.*

"Not only is it my *given* name, it's my *father's* name and his father before him. I'm actually Matt Matt, cubed."

"Well, Matthew Matthews the third, I have *volunteer* work to do, so if you don't mind," she said nodding her head to his body still blocking her path.

Matt stepped away, but never took his eyes

from her as she pushed her cart past him. Jane didn't look up.

"You're not getting off this easily, *Volunteer.*" He said the words quietly and the hair on the back of Jane's neck stood at attention. Perhaps it was the delivery of his line, or the calm nature of his silent promise to continue to pursue—whatever it was, it put Jane on watch and Matt Matthews on her problem list.

Without looking back, she moved along, trying to concentrate on placing a book on the shelf. When she turned the cart to make the corner at the end of the stacks, she glanced behind her. He was gone and instead of feeling a sigh of relief, she experienced something she'd not felt since she was a teenager—a trace amount of disappointment.

"SCARLETT?" STELLA STARED over the computer screen and into Jane's face. Recognizing her new identity immediately, she closed out the windows she'd been using to trace the Florida plate and sabotage the building's security system. Jane worked through a backdoor of the software used to store the library's surveillance footage. It had taken her longer than she wanted, but it was done. The cameras were on, but the daily backup file was now corrupt. Jane would be undocumented for at least thirty days when a routine security check of the building was scheduled. As for the plates, she had one, and only one, legitimate login and password. It was to the NSA mainframe. Any other logins were under assumed names buried deep with anonymous email addresses. Still, the plate came up to a stolen Kia Rio and not the black van. Jane was in no way surprised.

"Scarlett?" Stella repeated. Jane logged out of the library mainframe, using the login and password she lifted from Samuel Goodwin's desk while he sipped his vodka in the employee men's room. Being the only man on staff at Drake had its benefits.

"Yes."

"It's nearly one o'clock and you've not taken a lunch break. We'd hate to starve you on your first day."

Jane wasn't hungry. She was rarely hungry. She'd learned to survive on less than three meals a week as a child. The myriad of foster parents she'd had the misfortune of living with seldom used the money given to them by the government to feed and clothe the kids they'd taken on—except one—number ten—her very last foster home. Uncle Joe. At least that's what he told the kids to call him.

He was an older man—an Army Ranger vet who'd taught Jane how to fight off any unwanted attention or attack by a man, *or* woman, for that matter. He schooled her in the arts of Tae Kwon Do, Jujitsu, and marksmanship. Hearts and minds. It was what he'd taught her to aim for.

Pretty soon, what had started as weekend teachings and workout sessions turned into sparring every day after she'd finished her extra science homework. It taught Jane independence and confidence.

It was also Uncle Joe who'd purchase food for the kids in his keep each week, placing it in a dedicated fridge and cabinets in the basement. That food belonged to them. He didn't care how or when they ate, but it was all they got until the next Saturday afternoon. He was the best foster parent any of the five living with him had ever had. Jane was old enough at the time to realize how sad that was. Now, it was a distant memory. It wasn't the normal life of a teenager, but it was what she needed to equip her for the life she would someday lead. She didn't care it was different. And, she wasn't hungry.

Jane rose from the seat, putting the computer to sleep. "Sure."

She didn't bring her lunch, but there were free water bottles in the breakroom and Jane knew from the digital gauge on the wall it was sunny and seventy degrees outside—the perfect temperature to think.

Tugging open the combination lock, she dug her sunglasses out of her backpack, minding the loaded gun. She slipped the shades on her face and opened the refrigerator, noticing there was only one dog-eared take out box left out of the many Tupperware containers and paper bags she'd seen earlier. She assumed Sam Goodwin hadn't eaten his lunch either.

Jane walked out the back employee entrance and found a somewhat broken down bench sitting exactly where she wanted to be— in the sunlight.

The break area was surrounded by an old

chain-link fence entwined with overgrown weeds and twisted tree stumps. It was clear the city had scalped the area behind the building to keep the foliage from growing into the ancient power lines overhead. Jane was certain at one point the space had been a cozy wooded courtyard hidden from the bustle of the city. Now it was like a gutted animal—an open area exposed to the ugliness of the world.

Jane took a good long look around and deemed it safe for the moment. She sat on the bench and tilted her face toward the sun, soaking in its healing rays.

"So you're still here huh, *Volunteer*?"

Jane turned to find Matt Matthews leaning over the side of the mangled fence line, now *wearing* his aviators.

She stared at him through the darkness of her own sunglasses but said nothing.

"Seriously," he said, dropping his head for only a moment. "Are you going to tell me your name?"

"Why?"

"She speaks. Ladies and gentlemen, she has acknowledged me."

His jacket was hanging from his bag, his

shirt tight across his hard body. Sweat marks were beginning to form on his chest and underarms. He was the vision of a hard-working man. Rugged. Tough. Glistening. Jane took a deep breath and allowed her thoughts to meander to the sexual corner of her mind. What did Matt Matthews look like *without* his wrinkled clothes? She'd been on the move tracking two different assigned numbers for six months and it had been just as long since she'd been laid. An eager college student she met in a bar was the last man she'd used and it wasn't anything close to what she required of a one-night stand. Jane had since made a mental note to choose older, more seasoned men going forward. The last kid had great recovery time, but no stamina. Jane was a woman who had needs and desires—something a college boy had yet to discover in himself, let alone a woman. The good news was—he was more than accommodating when Jane left his apartment as soon as it was over, wanting nothing more than to use his bathroom before walking out the door.

"Hellooooo." He sang the word, trying to get Jane's attention which had wandered south to the bulge in his jeans.

She stood and pushed the sunglasses from her eyes to rest on her head. The brightness of the afternoon made her blue eyes sparkle and she read the reaction on Matt Matthew's face. Jane took a step toward him. "Jenkins. Scarlett Jenkins."

"It's a pleasure to finally meet you…*Scarlett*."

A moment of silence passed and Jane was thankful he didn't want to rehash the nature of her fake identity and its connection to the city they were in. "What are you doing back here?" she asked. "Stalking?"

Matt shook his head. "Happy accident. I'm not familiar with Atlanta. I thought I could cut behind the library to get to the next block without risking my life walking on the busy street."

One corner of Jane's mouth curled into a sarcastic smile. "Fear of traffic, Matt Matt?"

He gave her a lopsided grin, placing his own sunglasses on his head. "Maybe. I can handle bullets whizzing past me, but a car—not so much." He pulled his shirt sleeve over his elbow, revealing a long and jagged scar.

"Nineteen ninety-seven. A man who'd had a tough day at the office and an even tougher afternoon at the bar decided to drive home after one too many gin and tonics. I don't remember much except one minute I was walking home from school with my stylish Pokémon backpack, and the next I was in a ditch. I have another scar I can show you on my leg but I'd have to drop my pants."

Go ahead. Drop them.

"I was a little broken up. Missed the rest of fourth grade, I might add. It was a tragedy on many levels because Ms. Schneider was not only my favorite teacher, she was a babe. *And* I couldn't go on the class camping trip."

"Tragic."

"Yeah," he said with an amused shrug. "Well…you know…I worked through it with my shrink. Came out a stronger man on the other side."

Jane took another step toward him as he adjusted the satchel over his shoulder and noticed for the first time the windburn around his eyes. It was a familiar look—one only seen in those who'd been squinting in the sun and sand—and not on vacation. "Bullets whizzing?"

she asked.

Surprise crossed his face. "Did I say that?"

Jane nodded.

"I've been in the desert longer than I care to admit."

Jane digested his words and took another step toward him. "Deployed Service?"

"Journalist."

She took a step back and looked to her watch. "I need to go inside." Jane walked to the dented back door and placed her hand on the knob, thinking of all the journalists she'd met during active duty. Some were friendly, others, just a pain in the ass. Far too many of the reporters Jane encountered had put national security at risk just to break a story.

"Wait."

Jane opened the door, then turned to face him.

"What are you doing later? I mean, after you get off work—or—finish volunteering?"

"Why?"

"Jesus, you're making this hard, aren't you?" He looked to his feet for only a moment, then back to her. "I'd like to take you out for a drink."

"I don't drink."

"Coffee?"

Jane shook her head.

"Could we just hang out? We could just…you know…breathe. You breathe don't you?"

"I can't." Jane said the words and immediately slipped back inside, the cold air hitting her in the face. As much as she wouldn't mind having sex with Matt Matthews, it would never work. Jane already knew he wanted something she wasn't capable of giving. *More*.

DAY THREE | 2230 HOURS

JANE SAT IN the pizza parlor across the street from the warehouse. She'd ordered a small pepperoni but was served a large. The waiter apologized, then winked, bringing her a box. "Don't worry," he said. "It was my fault. I'll only charge you for what you ordered."

Jane had noted the time the restaurant closed, but asked the eager waiter anyway. "You locking up at eleven?"

The boy looked old enough, but was still fighting the signs of a ruthless puberty—the scars on his face told Jane he'd probably not had the easiest teenage years. "Yeah," he replied before allowing a long and awkward pause to linger. "Did you want to, you know, do something?"

Jane narrowed her gaze. She didn't want to hurt the kid's feelings—only because he was a kid. If he'd been even two years past his acne-riddled years she would been far more brusque. "Actually, Darren," she said, glancing at his nametag. "I wanted to sit and read for a while."

His already rosy cheeks filled with blood and he looked away before recovering. "Yeah, yeah. Sure. Of course. No problem. I'm closing tonight. You can stay until I lock the door. I mean, if you want."

Jane nodded.

Blotting the grease from her second slice of pizza, she watched for any sign of life across the street. An SUV had rolled into the loading area an hour ago. Jane noted the time. Since then, it was quiet. Too quiet.

She took a sip of water, opened her book and glanced at the words on the page but didn't read. Jane watched. Jane waited. Another half hour passed. It was eleven and the SUV drove away. Jane memorized the license plate. South Carolina 371 KKV.

The one light inside the warehouse was now off. The building looked like a haunted house with its dark wooden planks falling into disrepair. It was at least pre-World War Two, and Jane wondered how secure the building might be. She had a few tools in her backpack, but more than anything, Jane was resourceful. If there was a way into the warehouse, Jane would find it.

Dropping a five-dollar tip on the table, she gathered her hoodie and backpack as Darren clicked the lock on the door, allowing the last patrons to leave. Jane turned to pick up her book and found him standing in front of her.

"Leaving?"

Jane nodded.

Darren pointed out the window and across the darkened street. "I noticed you have an interest in the warehouse."

Jane looked over her shoulder at the dilapidated building and back to Darren without emotion. "Not really."

"It's actually a cool place," he replied, ignoring Jane's indifference. "Used to be an old tobacco warehouse. Then it was used by some t-shirt dudes, then a production company worked on their plays there. I think they may have even put on a show or two."

Jane nodded. Maybe Darren could serve a useful purpose after all. She gestured with her head toward the warehouse. "Looks to me like it's still in use."

"Not really."

Jane sized up Darren. Tall and gangly, she wondered what he was doing working so late. For someone so young, he seemed to know a lot about the buildings around him, which told Jane one thing. "Your parents own this place?"

"DeLuca's?" he asked, pointing to the tile floor beneath their feet.

Jane nodded.

"Grandparents."

"And the warehouse?"

"Yeah, they own that too. Here," he said pointing to the floor again. "Across the street," he continued. "And the Greek place next door."

Jane raised her eyebrows at the dichotomy of the two establishments, but didn't say anything.

"My grandfather is Italian. My grandmother is Greek. They both came from restaurant families."

Jane said nothing.

"Sorry. I'm rambling."

She shook her head, silently letting him know she didn't mind. "Do you know how long the lease with the current warehouse tenant is?"

He shrugged. "I dunno, but…" Darren turned on his heels and shouted. "Nonno!"

Jane leaned back to get a better look into the kitchen area.

"Si?"

An old man hobbled out of the back room and struggled to get his arthritic arm into what looked to be a *Members Only* jacket from the eighties.

"Nonno, this is…" Darren turned back to Jane. "I'm sorry. I don't know your name."

Jane looked to the balding man with the scraggly mustache and kind eyes. "Scarlett."

"Oh," Darren said with a smile. "Scarlett. Anyway, Scarlett was asking about the lease on the warehouse. Didn't you say it was short term?"

Jane gave the old man a nod and listened to him grumble derogatory words in Italian under his breath. "Month to month. I don't like him. Figlio di puttana."

"Nonno, *please*." Darren turned to Jane, a mask of embarrassment covered his face over his grandfather's obvious dislike of the tenants. Jane didn't care. She thought Thirteen was a sonofabitch too. "I'm sorry. He's just…"

Jane looked over her shoulder at the dark building. She wanted inside. "No. It's fine."

"You like see?" The old man's accent was as thick as the glasses on his face and he skipped words to get to his point. Jane understood him perfectly. He gestured to the dark warehouse with one hand and tapped his pocket with the other. "I have keys."

Jane stared at him. It was too easy. Too easy meant trouble. "Maybe." Jane paused and looked over her shoulder again at the building. "I don't want to waste your time."

"Ten thousand open square feet." The old man started his sales pitch. "Eccellente manifattura—*manufacture*. Dua toilette, tre porta. Cinque square foot."

"He said two restrooms—"

Jane cut Darren off. "Yeah, I got it. Two bathrooms, three dock doors, five dollars a square foot. Security?"

The old man shook his head. "But, you install," he said pointing to Jane.

"And the son of a bitch there now, did he install one?" Jane asked.

A smile crept across the old man's face and

he shook his head. "No."

Jane shrugged. "Okay. Let's take a look."

She waited outside on the sidewalk and stared at the warehouse while Darren and his grandfather turned out lights and locked up. They hadn't asked what she needed the space for. It seemed as if old man DeLuca was anxious to toss out Thirteen—that was, as long as he had someone else to pay the rent.

They crossed the empty street and Darren hung back. "I'm sorry if my grandfather seems, you know, *opinionated*. He's an old-school kind of guy. He does business in cash and on a handshake. He doesn't mean anything by it. He just has a low tolerance for people who aren't on the up and up."

Jane cased the outside of the building, never looking at Darren. "Your grandfather and I have a lot in common."

The three concrete steps leading to the entrance by the loading dock were crumbling. Old man DeLuca mumbled something under his breath and waved off the hunks of concrete lying on either side of the stair rail. The deadbolt groaned before snapping and the door opened with a push instead of a twist of the ancient doorknob. With a click of the light switch, the front of the warehouse illuminated.

"Merda." DeLuca muttered the word under his breath.

Jane agreed. The place did look like shit. She walked past them to get a better view of the papers lying across the three eight foot folding tables. Everything was in Arabic. Luckily, Jane could read it if the handwriting wasn't too sloppy. This time she didn't need to.

"There's an office in the back," Darren said, trying to move Jane along. It wasn't working.

The hair on the back of Jane's neck stood at attention and her heart rate dropped. She swallowed and stared at the acetone sitting in the corner behind the tables. She turned on her heels, tuning out everything the two men were telling her about the building.

If Thirteen was hoarding acetone, Jane knew other substances like peroxide would be in the building too. She needed to get them out and come back alone.

Quickly she looked for the back entrance she'd reconned two days ago. It was at the end of the loading dock area. She steered them both in that direction.

"Loading docks?" Jane asked the question and pointed. Her voice echoed through the space. Thirteen was using the warehouse as a staging area for his attack and nothing more. The place was virtually empty.

DeLuca nodded and pointed over Jane's shoulder. She hurried ahead of them and into the darkness. Scaffolding filled the back wall and Jane followed it with her eyes to the ceiling.

"Oh, yeah," Darren began. "The production group I told you about? They left all the ladders and scaffolding for their lights and stuff."

Jane looked away and Darren walked back to his grandfather who had called to him and was now cursing in Italian about the trash in the corner. It smelled like rotting food. Jane had smelled worse and shrugged it off, continuing to explore. She found the door at the end of the last loading dock and tried it, only to realize it opened from the inside only, the outside devoid of a lock or door handle. She pulled it open with a loud crack, and shoved a small piece of cardboard on the floor into the frame with her foot. Jane closed it with a push and walked away.

DeLuca spoke in broken English of when she could have the space. Jane didn't listen until he said it. *Ratto.* DeLuca was talking about the warehouse having rats. Now she understood the anger over the garbage.

"Scarlett? Scarlett?"

Jane finally turned to face Darren and his grandfather.

"Are you okay?" Darren asked.

Jane blanched. There was one thing she hated more than dirt. "Rats?"

"No-no-no." DeLuca frantically waved his hands.

Without emotion, Jane stared into the old man's face. If she were actually in the market for a warehouse, the rats would be a deal-breaker. "Thank you for showing me the space. I'll be in touch."

DeLuca shrugged his shoulders in disappointment and sent a steely glare toward his grandson. Jane knew he thought she'd wasted his time.

"Sure." It was all Darren could say.

Jane walked away and out the front door without saying goodbye. Behind her she heard

DeLuca say, "Voglio bruciare l'edificio." He was frustrated. He wanted to burn the building to the ground.

Jane began a slow walk down the street, her backpack slung over her shoulder. When she heard the two men locking the door to the warehouse, she turned and said, "Thank you, Mr. DeLuca." Her voice echoed over the empty street. He nodded in return.

Jane stood at the dark street corner. The neon Budweiser sign in the window of DeLuca's cast a blue shadow across her face. She pretended to wait for the stop light to change. As soon as the old man and Darren were gone, she was going back. Jane now knew the damage Thirteen was capable of. She needed to know how he planned to execute.

DAY FOUR |
ZERO DARK HUNDRED

JANE HUNG AROUND the alleyways listening to opera and waiting for the midnight hour, making sure the DeLucas were long gone and Thirteen and his crew weren't coming back. These people treated U.S. soil just as they would their own country—with suspicion. Lookouts were planted everywhere and they were expeditious in getting information back to their leader. They didn't trust each other, let alone someone from the outside, such as a landlord.

Aware of her surroundings, she moved to the back of the building, papering her lithe body to the side of the dilapidated wood. She took one giant step onto the loading dock and hustled to the door she'd compromised, careful not to disturb the chunks of concrete lying about.

Her fingers pried against the heavy metal. It was the one time in her life Jane wished she had the fingernails of a normal female. She spit into her hands and rubbed them together for a better grip. The rusty hinges cried out as Jane slipped an index finger painfully inside the metal frame deep enough to pry it open and duck inside before closing it, keeping the small piece of cardboard in the threshold.

Jane took a Maglite from the side pocket of her backpack and clicked it, illuminating the warehouse to a shadowy glow.

She moved through the old space in the dark by memory. She needed a better look at the papers on the tables. Making a mental note of how the sheets were arranged, she read through the pages in Arabic one by one, memorizing the details. Much of it was propaganda meant to keep the team on track. As she read her way to the bottom, she found it.

A plat map of the biggest park in down-town Atlanta. Architectural plans for the nearby headquarters of a soft drink empire and a national cable news network—all within less than a mile of each other.

"Holy shit." Jane couldn't keep the words contained inside her head. A coordinated attack, they were planning to blow all three simultaneously.

A wave of adrenaline overcame her as she stared at the date written on the map. Five days. Jane had five days to eliminate not only Thirteen, but to deal with the others prepared to assist in the attack. She couldn't eliminate his subordinates—Crow hadn't given her the kill assignment. But she'd have to deal with them all the same.

On the table beside the plans was the formula and a step by step instruction manual for TATP. Triacetone Triperoxide. Thirteen was making bombs. Three bombs. Known as the *Mother of Satan*, making TATP bombs *could* be as easy as baking a cake or as volatile as juggling live hand grenades. The fact they had instructions and weren't flying by the seat of their pants was unnerving. She stared at the workings of a well oiled machine. It had *his* fingerprints all over it.

Digging in further, she looked for Three's

name. Such a complex agenda would certainly have his blessing, if not his architectural seal of approval. She wasn't disappointed.

"There you are." She whispered the words and fell silent, taking in the enormity of what was before her. The man she wanted dead more than any other was right in front of her in black and white. A thrill overcame her. If Three was in the States, she could end him *without* a directive. But Jane wasn't a murderer. She was a trained operative working from direct orders *only*. As strange as it seemed, Jane considered it unethical to end the life of someone not in her mission directive. But *someone* wasn't Three. Jane had run the scenario of killing Three every day for as long as she could recall. If faced with the opportunity without an order, she was unsure of how she'd respond.

The significance of the mission was upon her at once. It wasn't what she expected. Her targets were never five days from executing their plan. They were weeks away—months. Jane always had time to plan and cover her tracks. Now, there were more people involved than her primary target, and there was no one to help her—not that she would ask. It was going to take ingenuity and planning on the fly.

A chill overcame her. A mumble of voices outside the main entrance of the warehouse sounded out in the dead night air.

Jane hurried to move the papers back into place and rushed into the darkest part of the warehouse—the back. The main door opened with a loud *clank*. Plastered to the wall in total darkness, Jane felt the scaffolding behind her. Turning in the pitch black, she began to scale the metal pipes littered with rags and two by fours until she was thrity feet above, staring down at the darkness below. The door opened. Light filled the bottom half of the warehouse. Jane lay face down onto a sheet of thin plywood at the top of the scaffolding, staring at her target through a splintered knothole large enough for only one eye.

The men begin to speak in Arabic. Jane held her breath, not making a move.

"What was the infidel doing in here?" the first asked. *"He has no right."*

They milled about the warehouse, making sure nothing had been touched. Jane watched the one giving orders intently. She waited for him to turn into the light so she could confirm his face, but the scarf around his neck continued to obscure his identity.

"*Take those with you*," the leader said, pointing to the formula papers and the plans of the three locations. He turned in a circle and stared at the acetone in the corner. Light fell across the features Jane had memorized from photos and footage of the beheading of a female journalist. Target confirmed. It was Thirteen.

The other two joined him at the tables. Jane strained against the small peep hole to ID them. Neither man was on *The List*. Thirteen had two unidentified associates: Tweedle A and Tweedle B.

Jane let out a painfully slow breath, her body motionless. She pressed herself into the sheet of plywood, desperate to be invisible. The fabric on her pant leg shifted and something tugged at the hem of her khakis. She turned her head, grazing her nose across the plywood, not making a sound. Silently she gasped. The matted and wet fur of a meaty rat came into Jane's focus as it climbed onto the back of her calf—its long and ropey tail audibly dragging along the plywood. Jane felt the weight of the hungry animal on her, its whiskers tormenting her skin as it inspected her exposed ankle and brandished its yellow fang-like teeth. Her eyes widened and she held in the frantic need to recoil—to kick it off—to kill it. She couldn't risk making even the slightest noise or she'd be found. Jane tensed. Swallowing hard she turned her face back to the men below. A second rat with a blood encrusted gash on its back nudged about her ponytail. The rats had been fighting each other for food. A third joined the first two, tap dancing on the plywood at her ear, its claws amplifying each high-pitch scrape. Jane closed her eyes and balled her fists. Her body tensed into a rigid state of horror as she desperately fought the urge to shake them from her body.

She pressed her forehead to the plywood, sweat now dripping from her temples. Jane clenched her teeth at their squeaks and hisses as sharp claws sorted through her hair and teeth nudged at the flesh of her ankle.

"*If the Italian infidel returns. Kill him,*" Thirteen shouted.

The lights cut. The door slammed. Jane kicked off two rats and shook the third, now deeply tangled in her ponytail to the concrete floor. Hearing them hit thirty feet below, she squirmed, trying to get the feeling of their grappling hooks off her body and out of her mind. Rolling back to her stomach, she belly-crawled to the side of the scaffolding and climbed down to the floor. Jane hurried to the back door, leaning her head into the frame, waiting for utter silence.

After three minutes of patiently standing by and continually shaking off phantom rats, she cracked the back door and listened into the dead of night before slipping out—covertly wedging the cardboard back into the threshold.

She walked two blocks in the wooded area behind the warehouse before crossing over the main drag that led back to her shoddy, but rodent free apartment.

Stopping across the street, Jane checked all four corners of the apartment complex for changes or activity. She counted the five cars in their usual spots and noted there wasn't a single light showing through the windows of Beverly Court.

She hurried across the street, climbing the steps two at a time. It was three in the morning and Jane was due to volunteer at the library at nine. She'd have just enough time to shower, catch a nap and take the Atlanta rail system to the heart of the city where the park, the cable company, and soft drink giant were all located. She wanted a first-hand look at Thirteen's targets.

Jane approached the front door and saw the shadow of footprints in the sand reflecting in the moonlight. Visually she cleared the area. When she was certain whomever had paid her a visit was gone, she stooped for a closer inspection. Three apartments away, the door opened and Melly walked into the night air barefoot and wearing the same threadbare nightgown.

"I told him you weren't here."

Jane stood. "You told who?"

"The man. There was a man knocking on your door tonight."

"What did he look like?" Jane moved in closer. "Do you remember?"

"Tall, dark. He wore a scarf."

"Wore a scarf where?"

"Around his neck—like Isadora Duncan."

"What?"

The old woman began to twirl in a circle.

Jane worried for a moment she would fall. "She's my favorite dancer," Melly said.

Jane took her by the elbow and steadied her footing. "Melly, tell me about the man."

The old woman shrugged. "What man?" A gnarled string of trim hung from the collar of her bedclothes, brushing her wrinkled cheek each time the wind kicked up. Melanie Munroe was as detached from reality as the lace was from her nightgown. "We'll talk tomorrow. After all, tomorrow is another day."

Melly waltzed to her apartment as if Fred Astaire was leading her across the dance floor and shut the door behind her.

Jane walked back to her own apartment and stared at the slight impressions in the sand. She wondered if Melly had really seen a man wearing a scarf. It was clear her thinking was muddy at best.

Jane inspected the imprints closely. Boots. Mostly likely a size thirteen. From the impression, Jane surmised he was tall but not heavy.

Sliding the key into the door, she opened her apartment, the smell of air freshener filling her head. The lamp she'd left on in the corner lit her way into the room. She locked the door behind her and slid the brace under the threshold, snapping it into place.

As much as Jane wanted to charge the doorknob with the camera, she worried Melly would wander out of her apartment to tell her something she remembered. Even the small shock the door would inflict could be lethal for a weak heart. She placed the camera on the kitchen table and walked into the bedroom, taking off her clothes as she went.

She scratched her head hard and drew blood, thinking of the rats. Jane could still feel their beady eyes watching her—their sharp claws scraping against her skin.

Looking into the cracked bathroom mirror, Jane noticed her dark circles. She brushed the bangs she'd cut herself out of her eyes and stared into her reflection, thinking of everything she'd learned tonight. She had five days. Five days to do recon on Thirteen and his two men. She knew if they were setting off three bombs, there was still another soldier of the caliphate who hadn't shown his face to her. Unless Thirteen was planning on detonating the suicide bomb himself.

She leaned into the tub, and turned on the hot water. Steam rose from the old, but clean porcelain. The mirror quickly fogged and she wiped it with her palm. Jane wondered who she really was anymore. "If Three shows his face, kill him and get out. Get out for good."

DAY FOUR | 0500 HOURS

R. WARREN WAS beaming when Jane's name was announced. Jane had put together the finest engineering project in her senior class with nothing more than a story from Uncle Joe's tour during Desert Storm and what she found lying about in his garage—including a 1993 Toyota Corolla.

When Joe Moretti waltzed, as he described it, into enemy territory in Iraq in 1991, he was, thanks to a rocket propelled grenade, trapped alive under a thousand pounds of rubble and concrete. He'd survived the ordeal, and his story gave Jane the big idea for her winning project.

An airbag system, made of rubber-reinforced Kevlar, each bag could inflate to twenty-seven psi and lift ten thousand pounds, utilizing reusable airbags that could fit inside a backpack with two small canisters of compressed air. Uncle Joe had told her during her many trials that she had to make it as light as possible. The *Battle Rattle* a soldier carried was already close to fifty pounds. Jane got her design down to exactly twenty and a half pounds.

Applause filled the school gym and Jane took to the stage, stunned and a little embarrassed. She didn't like being in front of crowds. She didn't like being noticed. Her fellow classmates teased her in a friendly way, always calling her MacGyver for the engineering projects she created from what she could find in junkyards and dumpsters. Jane only used what she found lying about. It had taught her how to be resourceful.

Mr. Warren handed Jane the small plaque. "I told you, your mind and ingenuity are your greatest assets. No one deserves this more than you, Jane."

She hugged the plaque to her body. It wasn't big, it wasn't special, but to Jane it felt like she held a world of possibilities in her hand. She stepped up to the podium and stared into the faces of her senior class—her engineering classmates all smiling at her in the first two rows of the gymnasium.

"I don't know what to say. I—"

The school bell rang out.

JANE OPENED HER eyes and slammed the stop on the alarm clock, the hammer bouncing between the two bells was too much to tolerate   at least this particular morning.

She rolled over in bed, sprawling spread eagled across the sheets. It had been a restless night of on-again off-again sleep. Jane knew she had a limited amount of time to accomplish her mission and it gnawed at her from the inside like the rats she'd encountered last night. She ticked the facts of the mission off in her head and it still hadn't come to her—the way she would take Thirteen down and put a halt to their plan. She had to figure it out soon. All she needed was a break, a lead, a stumble of some sort by Thirteen and his team. But Jane knew if Three was ultimately behind the attack, every aspect of their mission to kill had been carefully planned. Three was a diabolical killer with no remorse, but he was also a genius. It took one to know one.

Dragging her body from the bed, she sat on the edge and contemplated not running—she had too many other things she needed to do. Still, she stood and dressed and after her sit ups, push-ups and dips off the side of the bed, she stepped out into the cool morning air.

She counted the cars below and then descended the stairs to stretch her legs against the side of the old building before taking off into the darkness. The run would help to clear her mind. She needed to outwit the plan. And with a few days to go, she had no idea how she was going to accomplish it.

DAY FOUR | 0800 HOURS

JANE STOOD IN the center of the park. The wide expanse of green space and happy faces troubled her. Mothers and their babies strolled and stopped to play in the early morning hustle. City kids on their way to school were cutting through the park and joking around, teasing each other and playing tag. Runners were everywhere, lost in the world inside their earbuds and kicking it hard alongside the mothers with their jogging strollers. Fountains spilled water onto the pavements, the wind carrying sprays of mist into the air. Small children were wide-eyed, mesmerized by the beautiful day. In the distance, the letters of the network news station were emblazoned on the top of its tall building. The structure was two fourteen story office wings and a five hundred room hotel with a full height atrium—the target for the attack. Across the way, one of the country's favorite soft drinks had its corporate headquarters. It too, was a tourist attraction.

Jane dropped her head. The weight of the world rested on her shoulders in that moment. She stared at the ground, noticing a yellow dandelion fighting its way through a crack in the concrete sidewalk. She would've considered it a good sign, but Jane didn't believe in signs. Jane believed in doing her job.

The TATP bombs would be devastating— the worst attack on American soil in over fifteen years. The same bombs were detonated in Europe with horrific casualties—the death toll in the hundreds, the injured in the thousands.

Jane had deciphered from the papers that the attack was coordinated. The scenario would play out simultaneously—each explosion happening at the same time without a chance for authorities to clear the area. A suicide bomber would be planted inside a truck in the park. His counterparts in the sky high atrium and the lobby of the two corporations, which were also tourist destinations. Two times were given for consideration. Morning and after-noon—rush hour. Maximum damage. It was always the goal. Kill as many as many infidels as possible with the least amount of effort or resistance. To them, these innocent people were evil and disgusting, the lowest form of life. Thirteen planned to hit America in the heart—mothers, children, tourists and business people. Americans. Unbelievers. *Kafirs*.

She looked at the access area, mentally drawing a diagram in her mind, mindful of the location of the largest access road into the park. Jane took a deep and cleansing breath. The bombs weren't in place, but the clock was ticking.

She rushed down the street to catch the bus. She needed to get to the library early to run the plates she'd memorized and she wanted to log into the social media accounts of known recruiters. She hoped to ID the two unknowns in the warehouse last night with Thirteen. On rare occasions, she'd catch a glimpse of Three online speaking to boys of their obligation, doing his finest to twist the minds of young men. Her stomach turned each time she saw him, and yet she couldn't look away from the videos. Three wasn't just the mastermind of the attacks that killed people she cared about. Three was a full blown obsession for Jane. In the back of her mind she knew she would kill him or die trying.

"GOOD MORNING, SCARLETT." Doe Eyes sang out her words again. Jane found her, to her own surprise, a little less annoying each time she said it.

"Good morning, Rose *Marie*," Jane replied, careful to separate the two words.

She pulled the sunglasses from her eyes, the backpack from her shoulders and walked to the breakroom filled with beat up laminate folding tables and mismatched chairs. She secured her backpack in her locker, snapping the combination lock shut, tugging on it twice.

Passing Drunk Sam's office on her way back to the main area, Jane caught him in the act of taking a sip. It was eight forty-five in the morning. When Jane made eye contact with him through the crack in the door he'd left ajar, he did a spit take, spewing vodka across his desk.

Jane had two options. She could walk on as if she'd seen nothing, or she could confront him—blackmail him. Jane chose blackmail. "Mr. Goodwin." Jane pushed the door open. "I mean, *Sam*. Are you okay?" Before Sam Goodwin had a chance to wipe his mouth and make an excuse, Jane shut his office door behind her. "I'm afraid I can't let you go on like this."

"What do you mean?"

You can't smell vodka, was a lie alcoholics told themselves. Sam *smelled* of vodka, his office reeked of it and now his desk and the front of his shirt were covered in it. Still he refused to admit anything was out of the ordinary.

"Here's the deal. I'm not going to spill the beans on your drinking problem, although I suspect everyone knows. Call a cab, go home and come back after you've dried out, and by that I mean completed a twenty-eight-day program."

"Scarlett, I have no idea what you're talking about."

Jane sat on Sam's desk and leaned into him. "Yes. You do."

They stared at one another until tears welled in Sam's eyes. "You can't tell anyone, Scarlett. I'm begging you. My wife is leaving me."

"I'll make a deal with you." Jane stood and began to pace his office, hands behind her back like a drill instructor inspecting the barracks. "I'll get you a cab, because I can't let you drive," Jane said, taking the keys off his desk and placing them in her pocket. "You can leave through the back door. I'll tell everyone you're sick and going home. But...*you* are going to the nearest ER, checking yourself in and drying out. If you come back here any sooner than thirty days from today, I promise, I *will* out you."

Drunk Sam was now drunk, *crying* Sam. He nodded. "How did you know?"

"That you're an alcoholic? Or that you're gay?"

"Holy Mother of God." He dropped his head back in shock, covering his bloodshot and teary eyes. "How?"

"Look Sam, get the help you need so you can be an asset to the library and to whomever it is that you love—whether it's your wife or your boyfriend, it doesn't matter. I'm giving you a shot at a do-over. Take it."

"How did you know about Albert?"

"Let's just say I'm really good at reading people, Sam." Jane looked him in the eye. He didn't look away. She thought it was a good sign. "If you don't get the help you need, I *will* tell everyone *everything* I know. I have photographs of you stealing sips of vodka *and* of you kissing someone who isn't your wife." Jane lied. Neither of those things were true, but she knew Sam was lit up enough to believe her if she used an authoritative tone. Sam wasn't bad. He was an alcoholic. Jane wanted him to get the help he needed. Jane wanted him out of the library.

"I don't want to hurt anybody. I've hurt enough people."

Jane nodded. She'd backed into the room, issued a couple of ultimatums, made one huge assumption and was walking out with not only with the knowledge that she was right about Sam, whose lover's name she now knew was Albert, but also the keys to the library *and* his car. Ooh-rah.

———————

AFTER JANE LET everyone know the stomach flu had gotten the best of Sam, she told Stella his departing words were for her to be in charge. Stella immediately sat up in her seat and straightened the oversized sweater across her shoulders. "I can absolutely rise to the occasion."

"He knew you could," Jane replied, slipping off to the resource area of the library. Her goal was to find an unoccupied computer in a dark corner and log into social media sites to search for Thirteen's accomplices and Three. If he'd posted anything recently, Jane could possibly recognize the area from which he was filming. Three had a way of showing up, videotaping a message to his followers and disappearing again, as if he'd never been there in the first place. He, like Jane, was a ghost.

Making her way to the back, Jane spied an unoccupied public computer between the shelves of the musty stacks. The mildew smell alone was enough to keep everyone away.

She sat, and logged in using an access code now attached to another library patron's account. She could've used Sam's login and password again, but she didn't want the search history to come back and bite him in the ass. Sam had enough on his plate. If it came back to a middle-aged housewife, the FBI was less likely to send a dark van to sit in front of her house on a suburban street.

Logging into an online video service, Jane searched for Three's channel. It changed often as the site would shut down his account—usually by federal court order.

She pulled up the last known account and found that the *content was no longer available.*

"Shit." Jane grumbled the word under her breath.

"Profanity is strictly prohibited in the public library, Ms. Jenkins."

Jane closed the browser and stood, knocking the metal chair behind her over with a loud clank.

"Did I frighten you?"

Jane stared at him. He was wearing khakis, a grey t-shirt, boots and a shemagh—a scarf worn in the Middle Eastern deserts by soldiers to help protect against wind, sun, sand and cold. His sunglasses were propped on his head. "I don't *frighten,*" Jane replied.

Matt pulled the satchel he wore across this

body over his head, dropping it on a nearby table. He walked toward Jane, uninvited. "What are you doing all the way back here in the dark?" he asked. "Surfing porn?" His eyes sparkled when he smiled and Jane again wondered if his charm might translate into the bedroom.

Unruffled, she replied. "That would be against library policy."

Matt Matthews didn't look away and took another step toward her. "You know, you hurt my feelings yesterday."

Jane popped one eyebrow but didn't move.

"You don't believe me, do you?"

Jane said nothing.

"See, I'm *used* to asking beautiful women out to coffee and I'm *used* to getting a certain kind of response. Do you know what the others have said to me when I told them I'd like to buy them a drink?"

Jane squared her body and sat on the edge of the desk, crossing her arms before giving Matt Matthews an ear to ear grin. She shrugged her shoulders and summoned her sweetest voice. "Go fuck yourself?"

Matt lost his smile and narrowed his gaze.

"How'd you know?"

"Wild guess."

His mouth turned up in one corner and a sexy smile crept across his lips as he continued to move into Jane's space. "I'm a very tenacious man, Ms. Jenkins. You should know that."

"Tenacious?"

"Yeah," Matt began. "I don't really know what that means. I heard someone say it once."

"You're joking."

Jane didn't think it possible for the man's grin to widen. She was wrong. "I am indeed."

Jane watched Matt but didn't respond. His dark brown, curly hair lay in ringlets in the places he hadn't run his hands through. The sunburn on his neck and windburn on his cheeks told her he'd not been back in the States long. His casual nature and dress assured her he wasn't a man of great need. This wasn't a guy who came across as if he possessed a closet full of clothes and a fancy metrosexual apartment. Matt Matthews seemed to be more of an adventurer. Truth be told, he was exactly the kind of man Jane was attracted to sexually. Low maintenance. Genuine. Strong. The fact he seemed to have a tight muscular frame under that rumpled scarf and shirt was merely a bonus feature. She could only hope he wasn't a disappointment below the waist.

"I thought if perhaps I seemed helpless in the library, you'd, you know, *help* me."

Jane stood, never taking her eyes from his. She wanted to see if he'd look away, showing her his insecurities. He did not.

"What may I help you with, Matt Matthews?"

"You mean other than having a drink with me? Wait…I know, I know," he said putting his hands in the air in surrender. It was a look Jane liked on a man. "How about dinner. You eat, right?"

Jane stared at him without moving a muscle. He was so close to her, she could smell him. A mixture of soap and men's deodorant, he was turning on the side of her she kept deeply hidden until she needed, or more accurately, *required* a sexual release. Jane wasn't so much a ticking time bomb as an IED—tripped by the most unsuspecting of souls. Taking a deep breath, she calmed herself and asked a question. "Seriously, you must have a reason for coming to the library. What is it?

Because I know it isn't me."

He tilted his head and continued staring into her. "The truth?"

Jane nodded.

"The truth." He repeated the words like he regretted them and stared into the space behind Jane. "I'm kind of doing research. I'm just back from the Syrian border. I'm a freelancer and I'm on the trail of something—*someone*. I guess you could say I'm on my own—tracking. I'm looking for him and trying to find my dignity and reputation somewhere along the way. It's complicated."

The hair on the back of Jane's neck stood at attention. "What kind of research? You mean for a *story*?"

"Yeah, *a story*." Matt touched Jane's arm with his index finger. "And it's the kind of research you shouldn't tell people about—at least if you like them."

"Why?" She ignored the feel of his touch, uncertain as to whether it was intentional.

"Honestly, I could tell you who it is, but it wouldn't mean anything to you. Besides, I'm not in the habit of dragging folks into my screwed up world. It's not a pretty place. I do my best to keep it to myself."

Jane studied Matt's face. Who and what was this journalist looking for? Matt Matthews had turned from annoying to problematic. If he knew even a tenth of what was happening right under his nose in Atlanta, he'd win a Pulitzer. Still, Jane needed to find out exactly what Matt was up to. Jane took a chance that he'd want to brag and give her something. "Try me."

"S.D.K."

He gave Three's initials pausing between each letter for emphasis. Jane felt her heart stop cold. Her face went blank—vacant. She'd been searching for a lead to end Thirteen and his plan, and backed into a man who was tracking Three. Jane didn't shock easily and her muted facial expression translated to the outside world she was unaffected—lost. She was anything but.

Matt crossed his arms. "I told you it wouldn't mean anything to you."

She mouthed the word the first time, her voice too breathy to be heard. Jane cleared her throat and swallowed. "Yes."

"Yes what?"

"Yes, I'll have dinner with you. But I get to pick the place."

"Done. I'll pick you up at seven."

"I'll meet you there. Athenian Palace. It's in Five Points."

DAY FOUR | 1100 HOURS

JANE WATCHED MATT in the corner of the library, his lone notebook filled with God only knew what kind of facts on Three. She needed to get into his satchel, his mind, and his pants as soon as possible. After her completed mission with Thirteen, she'd be forced to evacuate. It was the plan. It was always the plan. She couldn't deviate.

When he continued to work in his little corner, Jane vacated the floor of the library, telling Stella she was leaving for a while—doctor's appointment. But Jane didn't leave. She locked herself in Sam's office. It was time to get to the bottom of who Matthew Matthews really was.

Keeping the light off, Jane worked by the light of the computer monitor. She started with a basic search, as she usually did. It was astonishing how much you could learn about a person from the digital footprint left behind with their social media accounts. Matt Matthews was too much of a player not to have photos online of his adventures.

A simple Google search brought up a business profile, part of a media service that linked business people together. His photo was old. Matt had aged quite a bit since he'd posted it or updated the information. She read through his unfinished profile. He'd gone to Carnegie Mellon in Pittsburgh—majored in journalism. There was one job title listed: reporter for the Miami Herald—not exactly the place for a war correspondent. There was one internship listed. Maxtronix, headquartered in Arlington, Virginia.

Maxtronix. Jane knew the name.

Opening a new window, Jane Googled Maxtronix and found the elaborate war defense website. Immediately clicking on the tab, *Our Team*, Jane found a lengthy bio on C. Matthew Matthews, Founder. Eighty-one when he passed away, the photo was of him as an older gentleman with grey hair and glasses, but the stormy eyes were a dead giveaway.

Jane let out a small gasp. "Holy. Shit."

Scrolling through to the CEO, she found Christopher M. Matthews II. She sat back in her chair for only a moment before moving on to the products. She already knew what she was going to find there—drones. Maxtronix was the number one supplier of combat mission drones to the United States Armed Forces.

"Holy. Shit." It was worth repeating. Matt's family was weapons manufacturing royalty. With a reported two-point-seven billion dollars in arms sales in the past year, they employed thirty-two thousand people and raked in over four hundred million dollars in profits.

Jane dropped her head into her hands. Why would a preppy rich kid surrender his cushy life of country clubs, tennis and weapons dealing with the U.S. government to live in a tent in the middle of the desert dodging bullets with the grunts? And now he's stateside and following Three. None of it added up.

She took a risk and went to the NSA mainframe, logging in with her username and password. Typing in Matt Matthews, she hit search just as she heard a noise outside Sam's office.

The hair on the back of Jane's neck stood at attention and she watched a shadow pause in front of the door. Jane put the computer to sleep and sat immobile, not making a sound.

She watched as the doorknob turned and then jiggled when the person on the other side found it to be locked. Jane heard the jingle of keys and held her breath. She was almost positive Sam had the only key to his office—almost.

After a few keys were tried unsuccessfully, the person walked away. Jane logged out of the computer, then waited a couple of minutes before sneaking out of Sam's office and into the break room for a bottle of water. She'd have to reserve further research on Matt Matthews for a later time.

DAY FOUR | 1500 HOURS

J ANE SAT IN DeLuca's drinking a water. She'd ordered breadsticks, but wasn't hungry. Still, if she was going to use her new Italian friend's place as a surveillance post, she needed to patronize the establishment. She did her best to focus on the mission at hand, but Matt Matthews continued to slip into her thoughts like a rising tide beyond her control.

Jane was alone in the restaurant with the exception of what looked to be a group of kids sitting in the back—eating pizza after their day at school—something she'd only read about in angst teen novels. Happy high schoolers who would hang out with their friends, spending a weekly allowance they did nothing to earn on pizza, movies, and lip gloss—driving new, or even hand me down cars, going to Friday night ballgames and school dances. It was all the rites of passage she never experienced as a teenager. Jane considered it a good school year if Social Services didn't show up in her classroom with a trash bag filled with her belongings.

Being pulled out of class to be shuffled to a new foster home with everything you owned in a Hefty bag wasn't something a kid forgot, and because of it, it Jane never really made friends—even in her magnet high school. She was *that girl*. The one the popular kids made fun of and the Bible beating kids wanted to save. Jane wanted to be left alone.

She sipped on a glass of water, and stared across the street—her Margaret Mitchell book in hand. She watched through the window, keeping track of any movement across the way, but there had been none—zero. Time was running out. She'd tracked the men to and from the warehouse each morning. In the afternoon, it was quiet.

All of the license plates had come back registered to cars and people who weren't in fact Thirteen, his band of killers, or the van they were driving. They were all stolen vehicles with traded plates.

"Back again?"

Jane turned to find Darren standing at her table, the white apron tied around his waist already soiled with red sauce. She nodded, but didn't say a word.

"Sorry about my grandfather last night. He's just…you know…*old*."

Jane waved him off. "It's fine."

A rowdy uproar of laughter came from the kids in the back of the restaurant and Jane leaned around Darren's body for a visual. The group got up in near unison, throwing their backpacks over their shoulders. The two boys and three girls were laughing and talking as they made their way to the front of the store.

"Let me know if you need anything," Darren said to Jane before walking away. Opening the door for the kids, he high fived one of the boys and smiled, nodding at the girls.

Jane looked back to the warehouse. She had four days to stop the attack. Four days. She'd yet to find a *real* schedule in the comings and goings of Thirteen and his two minions. Without a pattern, it was hard to plan a demise that looked natural or even accidental. And that was her charge. It was always her charge.

The bell on the front door chimed, and

Jane was caught off guard. The man entered quickly. Jane could only make out the back of his head.

Glancing back to her book, and then across the street once more, she heard the distinctive accent when his booming voice echoed into the empty restaurant. "DeLuca!"

Jane looked up from her book and caught her breath in silence. Thirteen.

Darren muttered his real name aloud in a breathy tone, unable to hide the fear in his voice. "I'm glad you stopped by. My grandfather wanted to speak with you about the trash in the warehouse. We've had problems with rodents."

Jane replayed the night before in her head and instinctively scratched her scalp.

"Tell your grandfather I don't appreciate him coming into the warehouse unannounced. I know my rights as a tenant and as such, he must give me notice that he is coming into the building. Do you understand?"

"I understa—"

"I know my rights. Do you hear me? I know my rights!" he shouted.

Jane pretended to be uninterested in the

kerfuffle. And yet she took in every nuanced word and action of Thirteen. He was an inhuman savage. A monster who had every intention of killing and maiming thousands of innocent people in four days. *Four Days.*

Jane memorized the Georgia plates of the silver Ford Truck as Thirteen drove away from the curb. She hoped to God they were legally registered, but she wasn't going to hold her breath.

She gathered her belongings and tossed a tip on the table for Darren. Before she had a chance to make her way out the door to the Honda Accord she drove, courtesy of Drunk Sam—the dark van that showed up every morning pulled into the loading dock. She tossed her backpack into the passenger seat and started the car. Jane waited to see if the van was staying, or if, per the usual, it would only make a pit stop at the warehouse. She wasn't disappointed.

One man exited the warehouse through the front door and climbed into the passenger seat. When they tore onto the street, she pulled out behind them, keeping a close but unnoticeable tail.

Three blocks later, they pulled into the parking lot of the Leopard Club—a famous strip joint known for their beautiful and fit women with *stimulating* dance moves. It was only a few years ago a fellow foster kid living under the same roof couldn't wait to age-out so she could audition for a position at one of their many clubs across the country.

Jane pulled into the fast food place across the street and took a parking place facing the road. She wanted full view of the men exiting the van.

One by one, Tweedle A and Tweedle B spilled onto the pavement and began their short walk to the darkened door of the club. It was three thirty in the afternoon, they were mere days from blowing themselves apart with a bomb and they were off to watch naked women dance for their enjoyment. Honestly, it was the one thing she could understand about these men.

Once they were inside, Jane crossed the street and parked the Accord in the space next to the van, careful Sam's plates were opposite the security cameras. Pulling the hood of her jacket over her head, she exited the car and walked around the van only once, hoping for a glance inside. The tinted windows shaded her view, but she could tell it was mostly empty other than hamburger wrappers and empty soda cans.

Jane cased the building and the busy street corner where the strip club was located. She spied an alley in the back and a couple of girls hanging out and taking a smoke break. Jane ducked into the drugstore next to the Leopard Club as Tweedle A walked out the back door and down the alley to chat up the girls.

Jane hid behind a colorful cling stuck to the window that urged people to get their flu shot. She watched his every move looking for something—*anything*.

When money exchanged hands, Jane knew not only were the boys dabbling in jiggle-joint carousing, they were dealing drugs. Thirteen and others like him fueled the billion-dollar business of trafficking opiates out of Afghanistan through Iraq. The more territory they conquered, the easier it was for them to smuggle drugs from town to town in the Middle East. Her guess was that Tweedle A and Tweedle B were also using the drugs to trade for sexual favors. In their eyes, their impending martyrdom in the attacks would wipe out any sin committed in the strip club.

They left abruptly, not paying attention to Jane's car when they loaded back into their van and drove away. Jane would have to wait for their return. It was a break—a small one—but still a break. She'd formulated a plan to take care of the two of them. She only hoped she had time.

DAY FOUR | 1700 HOURS

T HE SUN BEAT down on Jane and seven of her fellow Marines. In a small town in the Euphrates River valley, they were deep in the heart of Islamic State territory. An Expeditionary Task Force, the team of elites had landed in choppers and spent the better part of the afternoon sweeping the area for captives—looking for bodies.

Another soldier shouted from atop a mound of rubble one hill away. "We've got a convoy approaching!"

Jane heard the command over the radio and took cover, setting up a strikepoint from ten yards out. As the convoy approached the passenger was identified over the radio. An Islamic State militant the U.S. military had hoped to capture and interrogate had landed right in the hands of Jane's unit.

It started out as civil as the conversation between a Marine taking a soldier of the caliphate into custody could be, but soon turned deadly.

Jane felt beads of sweat roll from her temple. She didn't flinch, keeping the two jihadists in question inside the crosshairs of her sight. Jane was unsure who fired the first shot. She didn't care. A firefight broke out. From her post ten yards above the action, Jane fired two shots into the head of each of the terrorists. They fell, collapsing like ragdolls into the sand.

Jane took a deep breath and watched the second vehicle already bugging out and driving into the desert before rolling onto her back. She stared into the blazing sun and let out a sigh of relief.

Her fellow Marines cheered for her and hurried to patch up the one wounded man in her unit. A graze to his arm, even he cheered for Jane.

"Get some JD!" one of them shouted.

Standing, Jane tried to suppress her smile. She couldn't. Instead she waved them all off. "Yeah, yeah, yeah."

It was a wonderful moment. A proud moment. She was one of only two women in her unit and the boys' club hadn't made it easy for her or the other female soldier, Jennifer Drenkowski, to prove themselves. Today, Jane was chalking one up for the JDs even though Jen was back at basecamp. She missed patrol to give an interview to one of the bigger newspapers on women in the military. Jane had declined the offer.

"Let's move the fuck out of here!" Jane's C.O. shouted.

Jane turned to leave, still high from the mission. The air left her lungs. She felt herself falling, staring into the face of Jennifer Drenkowski. The whites of Jen's eyes were red with blood and a despondent look covered her face like a mask. Jane suddenly felt heavy. Heavy with darkness. Heavy with sadness. Heavy with death. Jennifer pulled Jane's face to hers, their hands shaking with adrenaline. The last gasp of life left her fellow Marine and best friend's body as she whispered the words, "Help me."

Jane shot up from the bed fighting for air. Her gun locked and loaded in her grip "No?"

She took three full breaths, swinging her

legs over the side of the bed. She hadn't dreamt of Jen in months. The idea of Three being so close was stirring up emotions she'd never fully dealt with.

Turning on the bedside lamp, Jane picked up her backpack from the floor beside the bed where she'd dumped it before closing her eyes. Pilfering through the few items in the bag, she found it. A tin box that once held sore throat lozenges, secured by a thick rubber band, it contained everything Jane held dear.

She sat on the bed, placing the tin in front of her. She'd carried it with her everywhere as long as she could remember. Its contents were strange and yet not out of the ordinary. She slipped the tight rubber band from the box and set it aside. The hinges were rusty from its time in the desert, and Jane could still feel a few grains of sand in the bottom each time she sorted through it.

Inside there were two photos, a diaper pin with a pink head, a sixpence, a red ribbon, a dog-eared and redacted police report and one Marlboro cigarette. To anyone else, it would look like a pile of junk. To Jane, it was her everything. It was her life.

Placing the photos side by side, she stared into the face of Jennifer Drenkowski and fingered the cigarette.

Jen was the first real female friend Jane ever had. The first one she'd ever trusted. They'd suffered through the Marine Corps together, side by side—sticking together like glue. Jen always had her *six* and Jane had hers. It was a running joke that they looked alike, acted alike and had the same initials. The men thought it was funny, Jane and Jen thought it was divine intervention—at least Jen thought so. They had one difference. Jen was a smoker. She'd once told Jane that smoking was the only thing that made her feel normal in their fucked up world. Jen tried her best to get Jane to join her—even gave her a Marlboro Light to hang onto. Jen's words were, "Someday you're going to need this, and I wanna be there when you finally smoke it—even if it's just in spirit."

Jennifer Drenkowski and Jane were too similar—so much so that when a bounty went out on Jane's head for killing two of Three's senior men that day—Jen was killed. Executed by beheading, they'd raped and tortured her— and filmed every moment.

Jane ran her finger across the photo. "You big dummy. Why'd you go and let yourself get captured? It should've been me," she whispered. "It should've been me."

She stacked the candid photo of Havis on top of it and packed her Sucrets tin up with care, wrapping the rubber band around it before tucking it back into her bag.

Glancing at the clock, Jane knew she needed to hit the shower if she was going to make it to her dinner with Matt on time.

Jane had every reason to want revenge, but she was more interested in justice. She wouldn't stop until she had it.

DAY FOUR | 1845 HOURS

MATT FOUGHT WITH himself, sitting in the parking lot of the rundown apartment complex that was Beverly Court. Did he show up at her door for their date, unexpected? Or did he follow her orders, and meet her at the Greek place? He wrenched the rearview mirror in his hand to get a better look at himself. The dark circles under his eyes were more prominent than usual, but he'd had a hard time sleeping since he'd rolled into Atlanta via Pittsburgh, where he'd stopped at his condo only long enough to shower and pick up his car.

He had fifteen minutes to change his mind and still make it to the sandwich shop on time. The question was, did he want to? He glanced at his reflection one last time before putting the mirror back in its correct position. The answer was, no. He'd asked her on a date—a proper date—not one of his usual *Netflix and Chill* escapades where he wished the chick would leave or turn into a pizza after they'd screwed. Matt had fuck buddies in lieu of relationships, and even those were as hard to come by as pizza in the middle of the desert.

He leaned forward, looking into the sun at her apartment door and wondered if he was doing the right thing. Matt had a lot at stake at the moment—a lot of irons in the fire—it would be unfair to ensnare her into his tangled web of deceit.

Matt reached for the door as his pocket buzzed. His phone was on silent, but he noticed the display before he answered. *Unknown Caller.*

"Matthews."

There was a long pause and for a brief moment, Matt thought perhaps the call he'd been patiently waiting for had finally come through.

"Hello?"

A series of clicks on the line told Matt one of two things: the call was either being traced or it was a secure line.

"Matthew. It's your father."

Secure line.

He hesitated before responding. It had been months since they'd spoken. For Matt, it wasn't long enough. His response was hushed and indifferent. "Hello, Dad."

Matt endured the pregnant pause that followed as long as he could, then finally spoke again. "How are you?"

"I'm glad you made it home safely, son. I'll bet it feels good to be back on American soil."

It was Matt's turn to go silent. There was nothing he wanted to discuss with his father. For now, he was forced to play along—to be the *good son.*

"How long have you been back?"

Matt leaned his elbow in the open window of his car, resting his head in his hand. "Couple of weeks."

Another lull took over the discussion, but Matt refused to do the heavy lifting in the conversation. After all, it was his father who'd called him. That meant he wanted something. Christopher Matthews *needed* something.

"Any plans to come home?"

"I've already been home. I flew into Pittsburgh and picked up my car." Matt gave his explanation, but he knew his father was more than aware of where he'd been. Christopher Matthews always knew where his son was.

"I meant to the business in Virginia—our home in Maryland."

Matt knew making that distinction was a sticking point with his father, but when he'd left home at eighteen for college in Pittsburgh, he never looked back. And he never came back. He wouldn't be back now if the current situation wasn't forcing his hand. "I knew what you meant. Look Dad, there's nothing for me in Virginia *or* Maryland."

"*Nothing?*"

Matt could only be respectful to a certain point. They didn't share the usual father-son relationship and although Christopher Matthews was a philanthropist and a do-gooder to the outside world, Matt knew exactly who his father was. And he didn't like him. At twelve, he didn't like the fact his father cheated on his mother while she lay in a hospital bed dying of breast cancer. Chris Matthews thought his son was too young to understand what was going on. He wasn't. Matt didn't like the fact that his father had taken the upstanding defense research and development company his grandfather built after the Korean War and twisted it into a business more focused on making money than helping keep our military safe. Matt Matthews' feelings for his father verged on hatred. He wanted to care about his father, but now that he'd seen his dad for who he really was, he *couldn't* care. He *wouldn't* care. For now, he played along. Biding his time. "You know what I mean, Dad. I go where there's a story."

His father scoffed. "Stories? This is D.C. We live in the middle of *all* the stories. Besides, you've had your fun trekking all over the world writing or whatever."

The last word did more than just get under his skin—it dug deep into his flesh. Matt looked to his watch then ran his hand through his thick waves. "Look Dad, I'm late. I've got a—I'm late for an appointment."

Another long pause took over the conversation and Matt was tempted to hang up. He didn't.

"I'd like for you—" His father began and then stopped himself to calibrate his request. "It would mean a lot to me if you would consider coming home—I mean, if you would consider coming back to Virginia to work at Maxtronix. It's a family business, Matthew. And even though you and I don't always see eye to eye, you *are* family."

"I'll think about it." He lied. In the end, Matt knew he'd have no other choice.

Christopher Matthews made a grunting sound on the other end—one of the many weird noises Matt had learned to interpret over the years. This grunt was one of careless surrender. Chris Matthews had washed his hands of his son. He just wouldn't admit to it. It would be bad for his good-guy image. "I guess I can't ask for more than that," he said. "We'll talk again soon."

"Bye Dad."

Matt ended the call and sat back in the leather seat of his freshly cleaned car. He wasn't about to let his father ruin his night. He took another look at his watch. It was too late to back out and drive away. She would be walking out of her apartment at any moment.

Matt climbed from the car and took the stairs two by two to the third floor. It was time to be charming for Scarlett Jenkins.

DAY FOUR | 1900 HOURS

JANE STARED IN the bathroom mirror. She put the yellow cardigan over her white t-shirt then took it off again. She was a woman with very little in the closet, and even less to wear out on a date. Her dinner mission as far as she was concerned was two-fold: find out who Matt Matthews was and what he knew about Three. Last, but still gnawing at her insides, was the chance to get laid. She rolled the idea of having sex over in her mind, took off the t-shirt and put the sweater back on, unbuttoning the top two buttons to show a necessary amount of cleavage to catch Matt's attention. If she wanted him to look at her as a woman, she needed to look the part.

Three knocks came at the door. Jane pulled the gun behind the toilet in a fluid motion, locking and loading without thinking. Autopilot. *Always alert. Always prepared.*

She hurried to the door without a sound. Three more knocks.

"Scarlett? Scarlett, are you in there?"

She peeked through the space between the curtain and the window and found Matt Matthews rocking back and forth on his heels. A twinge of adrenaline filled her veins and Jane's pulse quickened. "Who is it?" she called out, buying time to get rid of her gun.

"It's Matt. Matt Matthews?"

She rolled her eyes at his nervous tone and opened the nearest kitchen drawer, dropping in the loaded weapon before cracking the door, keeping one foot inside to block an unwarranted entry.

Matt was dressed in a pressed pair of khaki pants, white button down and boots. He wore the same shemagh scarf and his army green field coat. Jane cocked her head. "What are you doing here?"

Matt looked dumbfounded by her initial reaction. "I ah…well I—" he stopped midsentence, noticeably waiting for Jane to pick up the conversation. She didn't.

"We have dinner plans."

Jane was silent.

Matt grimaced and shrugged his shoulders, rolling his eyes back in his head. "I'm sorry?"

He issued his apology in the form of a question and searched the sky. He shoved his hands deep inside the pockets of his starched khakis. He was visibly nervous. "I can explain."

Jane grabbed her backpack and walked out, closing the door behind her. Matt stepped away and she glanced to their feet. The boot prints matched those she'd memorized from her visitor before. Jane didn't take a beat before realizing the truth. The man in the scarf Mellie told her about was Matt.

He held his arm out for her to walk ahead. Jane obliged him and counted cars—seven. The usual five clunkers, Drunk Sam's Honda Accord, and a vintage navy blue BMW that stuck out like an Ivy League preppy at a tractor pull.

Jane walked to his car without prompting and he opened the door for her before she had a chance to do it herself. She climbed inside and began to look around the interior. It was freshly cleaned as evidenced by the vacuum marks on the tan floor mats. There was loose change in the cup holder and an extra pair of sunglasses tucked into the visor. The car smelled of old leather and money. Matt started the car and placed his arm on the back of Jane's bucket seat. Jane looked straight ahead but felt his stare across her *necessary* cleavage.

"Are you going to give me the silent treatment all night?"

Jane looked to him and blinked.

"Fine. I picked you up at your apartment because I wanted this to be a proper date and not just two people meeting up and hanging out." Matt took a long deep breath as if he was trying to calm himself. Jane remained quiet. "You can't stay mad at me *all* night, can you?"

"If I were *mad*, I wouldn't be in the car with you. How did you know where I live?"

Matt backed out of the small parking lot and put the car in drive. "That's a fair question. I followed you on an early morning run the other day."

"What?" Jane stared at him. She was a trained operative that could spot a tail from a mile away. How could she have missed him?

"I'm sorry. I was up early for a run and there you were. I just...I dunno.... followed you. And don't ask me why, because I have this thing where I always have to tell the truth. I can't lie. I mean I can, but I'm so bad at it it's better if I tell the truth. It keeps me from looking like a douchebag."

Jane subtly pursed her lips. "Why?"

Matt Matthews let out a heavy sigh as they came to a halt at a red light. Jane watched him squint his eyes and wrinkle his nose as if making a face would make his next sentence more palatable. "Would you be upset with me if I said I liked watching you from behind?"

"You expect me to believe you recognized me running, then followed so far behind I didn't notice. All the way to my apartment?"

"Not exactly. I watched you running first, and then I met you at the Library. When you walked away with your book cart, it didn't take long to put two and two together." Matt knitted his brow. Jane knew the look. His glib expression was erased by his curiosity. "Is that so hard to believe? I *am* an investigative reporter you know. I'm smooth, Scarlett— smooth like a baby's bottom. I can be a ghost when I wanna be. I learned a few tricks out in the field from my buddies in the Marine

Corps."

Jane wanted to say at the very least, he'd hung out with the right people in the desert, instead she asked a question. "Wanna explain what you were doing at my apartment *last night?*"

"What?" The word came out breathy, his astonishment on display. His face told her he *knew* he was made. "I ah—I thought you might be home. But…you weren't."

Jane said nothing.

"It was late. Where *were* you?"

She ignored the question. Jane didn't answer questions, she asked them. "Where are you going? You just missed the turn to the Greek place."

At once, Jane was on alert, one hand inconspicuously on the door handle, the other on the back pack at her side. She wasn't afraid to jump from the car if she needed to.

"I picked another restaurant. Is that okay?"

"I thought we agreed on the Greek place."

He came to a rolling stop at the next red light and turned to her. "Is everything okay, Scarlett?"

Jane looked him in the eye, but didn't say a

word.

"I never meant to upset you. Really I didn't. I just wanted to take you to a nice restaurant for dinner. Someplace that doesn't have paper napkins. Is that okay? I mean, I can turn around and we can go to the Greek place. We can do whatever you'd like. I want you to be happy. If you're happy, maybe you'll stop giving me the death stare."

"Fine." Jane loosened the grip on her backpack. She nodded and looked straight ahead. "And I'm not giving you a death stare."

Matt let out a nervous laugh. "I know a death stare when I see one."

"Then you've obviously never seen a dead person."

Matt popped his eyebrows. "Wow."

Jane stared straight ahead.

"You think I'm a cupcake—that I'm soft. Don't you?"

Jane didn't reply. She thought he was handsome, had a nice body and if he was buying dinner and stopped talking so much, she might crawl into his bed and rock his world for a couple of mindless hours before rifling through his head to get his back story.

"Look Scarlett, I have nightmares—horrible nightmares. I've seen good men blown to pieces. I've watched children die. There's not a day goes by I don't jump or duck when I hear a loud noise, and God forbid a car backfires. Is that what you wanted to know?"

Jane didn't reply. She understood post-traumatic stress disorder. A lot of foster kids suffered from it. Not because of witnessing death and destruction, but because of the physical and psychological torture they were subjected to. You didn't become a foster kid because your life was wonderful. You became one because your life was shit.

Jane was an early victim of PTSD. She'd turned the feeling of fear on its head when rage and revenge took over her soul by the time she turned sixteen. Uncle Joe helped her to focus her fury into something positive—the ability to defend herself. Mr. Warren helped her focus the same emotion to escape the life she never wanted to come back to.

She could appreciate Matt's feelings, but she no longer identified with them, and sympathy wasn't one of her strong suits—at least not toward a grown man who'd so obviously enjoyed a cushy life—even if he *did* choose to be a reporter in the Middle East.

"Look, Scarlett. I don't want to spend the night begging you to talk to me. I can take you home if you'd rather. Otherwise, I'm gonna need you to at least *act* like you want to be here."

"We can use real napkins."

"And?" Matt asked, looking at her in between watching the road in front of him.

"Look, I'm not one of those bubbly girls. I don't flip my hair and giggle. That's not me."

"I could get one of *those* anytime I want. Not to brag, but they practically throw themselves at me in bars. I like real. I like— genuine. I like it that you *aren't* one of those girls."

Jane bit her bottom lip. Matt seemed like a nice enough guy but she spent most of her life pretending to be anyone but herself. How could she ever be genuine? Still, if she wanted to know who Matt really was and why he was tracking Three, she needed play nice. That meant playing along—playing her part. "I've had a bad couple of days," Jane replied. "Thank you for sharing that you have PTSD. I know that's difficult to deal with, let alone talk about with a complete stranger."

Matt showed Jane a somber grin letting her know it *had* been hard for him. "Maybe after tonight we won't be strangers, Scarlett Jenkins."

Jane gave him a nod and said, "Okay." But she knew even after tonight, they *would* be strangers. No one *really* knew Jane.

He pulled the car into a parking space and killed the engine. Jane looked over her shoulder and found a trendy-looking bar and grill—the kind of place young thirtysomethings hung out to discuss politics, craft beer and wind surfing in places like Bora Bora. These were all topics Jane felt certain Matt was well-versed in. The problem was, Jane, for once, didn't mind being in the company of a man who'd so obviously had a carefree existence up until he thrust himself into the world of reporting. She thought perhaps that was why she'd accepted him. There was something admirable about deliberately putting oneself in the middle of a shit storm. Sure, she wanted to know what he knew about Three, but somehow it was more than that. Jane couldn't put her finger on precisely what or why that was. But she was willing to do her due diligence.

Out of the car before he was, she waited for him at the door of the restaurant.

"You're quick on the draw, Scarlett."

"You have no idea."

DINNER CONSISTED OF dishes with fancy names put together by a famous chef Jane had never heard of, nor cared to. Still, the food was excellent and the company better. The only time Matt seemed to question her was when she'd requested to *not* sit with her back to the restaurant. He'd laughed, but Jane needed to be ready to kick over a table and shoot if need be. *Always prepared. Always alert.*

Matt told her of his four years in the Middle East. Jane ate deliberately, thankful for the meal. It was something she'd learned long ago. She chewed slowly while he relived the antics of living and partying with other reporters while they put in the time, searched for leads and stayed out of the line of fire. Jane saw through his privileged kid denial, especially when he explained how he didn't want to go into the family business—although he'd failed to mention it was a *multibillion dollar* family business. Jane stayed away from the obvious questions, hoping he would give up information on his own. She never wanted to ask directly for the answers she sought. It was always better if she put the other person at ease and lured them into telling her what she needed to know. She'd wait for the answers to come naturally. And they always did.

"We've made it through dinner and I still don't know what you're doing in Atlanta, Scarlett? Is this your hometown?"

Jane shook her head and took a sip of water. "I think the more interesting question is why are *you* here? You're just back from the Middle East. You're looking for a big story but why here? What could possibly be in Atlanta, Georgia?"

"When did I say I was looking for a story?" He wiped the condensation from his glass nervously.

Jane looked him in the eye, the light of the candles casting a yellow glow on the face of the golden boy. "You're looking for a story to take you back to your glory days and you need it soon because the last thing you want is to ask your family for money. That's why you're living in the same part of town I am, and not in some trendy, high-class place like Buckhead." Jane paused and looked around her. "What'd you say? You're hoping to find your—*dignity*? It's complicated, you said, but I think that's how you phrased it."

Matt Matthews was quiet for the first time all night. He looked away—anywhere but into Jane's face and she realized summing people up like a suspect ID sheet didn't come across in the no nonsense manner she intended. Jane didn't *people*. She knew it.

"I'm sorry." They were words Jane didn't use often. Sorry was for people who had regrets. She had none and the phrase felt unusual crossing her lips.

Matt swallowed hard before looking her in the eye once more. He shrugged his shoulders. She'd hit a nerve. "It's fine."

Jane leaned into the table. "I didn't mean for that to come off like—"

"Like you're an asshole?"

Jane bit her lip, holding in a rare smile. Matt Matthews' stock rose in an instant. "Yes."

"Look, I know you're not an asshole, but you're standoffish as hell."

Jane stared at him and said nothing. She took his words as a compliment. She prided herself on never getting involved with people. People were trouble and trouble was something she didn't need in her life. Still, she didn't look away.

"And yet, you have this unnerving way of making me feel like *I'm* the asshole, when you're the one …you know…" Matt's voice trailed off.

"*Being* the asshole?"

"Well…. yeah. You remind me of this guy I once knew. General Painswick. Jesus, that guy could stare you down and make you feel like a piece of shit. And he didn't even open his mouth to do it. It was just that *look*. Suddenly I was five years old and my mother was staring me down—you know, back when you were deathly afraid of your parents and getting in trouble was the end of the world?"

No. Jane didn't know. But she knew *Bring the Pain* Painswick—the peanut butter eating sonofabitch with no conscience. "When were you in Iraq?"

"I never said I was in Iraq."

Jane realized she'd asked without thinking. She wasn't good at idle conversation and she'd jumped the gun with her questioning. She covered. "Of course you did."

"When?"

"When you were harassing me in the courtyard behind the library. The day we first met."

Matt narrowed his gaze. The look told Jane he wasn't buying it.

Matt took a sip of his water, his face now filled with the confidence she'd witnessed upon their first meeting. "I know I didn't tell you I was in Iraq," he said. "I would've said *Middle East.*"

Jane shook her head and pursed her lips. It was time to tap dance. "Nope. You said Iraq. How else would I know that?"

Matt shook his head slowly back and forth without taking his eyes from Jane's. She could see the wheels turning in his head and was thankful when a bouncy waitress with big boobs showed up at the table.

"Hey y'all. I'm Amanda. Your server, Jim? Yeah, well, he wasn't feeling so hot, so I'm taking over his tables." The bubbly blonde turned her attention to Matt immediately and completely. "Can I get you anything else?"

Matt nodded to Jane.

She raised one disapproving eyebrow at Matt before giving Amanda the pleasure of her drink order. "I'll have another soda."

"Diet soda?" Bouncy Boobs lost her innocent smile.

"Did I say diet?" Jane paused, giving Amanda's backside a noticeable once over.

"Regular soda," the waitress said in a huff, losing her toothy grin before turning her attention to Matt. "And for you?"

"Same."

Boobs walked away and Jane looked up from her lap to find Matt grinning at her from ear to ear. "What?" she asked.

"That was impressive."

Jane shrugged. "I've dealt with girls like that my whole life. I'm sure deep inside there's a nice person trying to get past all the self-centered bullshit she's wrapped herself in."

Jane reached inside the pocket of her backpack, laying her free and open hand on the table. With care, Matt cradled it, sandwiching her fingers between his two warm palms. The heat from his body radiated across her skin.

"And what are you wrapped up in, Scarlett? Deep inside?"

Jane pulled away, catching him off guard.

"Wow." Matt's face was flush with embarrassment and he sat back in his chair.

Jane made a production of showing him the hand sanitizer she was retrieving from her bag.

"Oh." He let out a nervous laugh as Jane squirted a glob into her palm. "Did you do that because I touched you?"

Jane stared into his face. Matt Matthews was a decent enough guy. She needed to find out what he knew about Three, put him on a different trail and get him out of harm's way before she terminated Thirteen and dealt with his crew. She hadn't decided if that meant having sex with him or not.

"I was in the process of getting it from my bag when you grabbed me."

"I didn't *grab*." His voice had the perfect mixture of frustration and flirt. "Your hand was there, so I *held* it."

Jane studied Matt, but didn't respond. The thick dark curls on his head were sexy and reminded her of a time long ago. She'd shared a night of *lust and thrust* with a fellow Marine once while on leave. He had the same kind of thick waves. Jane remembered three things about him: He asked her to say his name while they screwed—Tony. He'd wanted her to run her hands through his hair—she did. And his body was blown apart by an IED while on patrol two weeks later.

Jane put her freshly sanitized hand back on the table palm up, ready to be held. Matt ignored the gesture, pulling his phone from his pocket to check his notifications.

Jane took her hand away.

Perky Tits was back with their sodas. "Anything else?"

Matt gave a nod across the table, silently reaffirming the question. Jane shook her head, and the waitress left. She feared she'd screwed up the evening with her obsessive compulsive hand sanitizing. "I used the sanitizer because Perky Tits said our waiter went home sick and I don't like germs. Would you like some?"

Matt gave her a half-hearted smile. "Perky Tits?"

Jane shrugged. "I don't use people's names very much. I just...I give them more of a descriptive moniker.

"Really? What's mine?"

Hot Journalist. Writer guy with the nice bulge in his pants. My next horizontal tango. Man I need to recon. She shrugged her shoulders and lied. "I don't have one. *Yet.*"

He smiled at her and for the briefest of moments, Jane forgot the one thing that never left her thoughts, Three. She'd agreed to have dinner with Matt for two reasons. To find out if he knew anything about the man she wanted to kill, and to get laid. She needed to turn it around quickly, so she chose a subject she knew nearly everything about as a litmus test. If he didn't play hero for just being there, she'd sleep with him. "Did you go on any exciting missions in the Middle East, *not* Iraq?" she asked with a joking smile.

Matt scoffed and took a drink of his soda. "It was ugly—a hell hole. I sat on the sidelines and it was ugly. Say what you will about our U.S. military, those guys are badass." He shook his head and looked away. Jane could see him reliving his experience. It was the thousand-yard stare, and it was easy to spot on anyone who'd been there. "And the Marines..." Matt continued.

"What about them?" Jane asked, softening her face.

"I don't know that I've ever met a tougher group of men."

"Or women," Jane quickly added.

He nodded. "Yes. Or women."

"You mentioned a name the other day," Jane said hoping to spark the conversation about Three. "Was *he* a Marine?"

"Siad al Daleel ul Khyayraat."

Just the sound of his name sent a pang of rage through her core. "You called him something else."

"SDK."

Jane nodded. "I can see why you don't use his real name."

"They call him The Instructor."

"*The Instructor*," Jane repeated in a whisper. She looked away, Three's face flooding her mind.

Matt stared at his soda, wiping the condensation off with his fingers. "He's the kind of guy who kicks puppies for fun." He brought his gaze to Jane's eyes. She knew he wanted to drive home his point. "He does worse things to his *real* enemies."

I know. "Such as?"

Matt took a breath and looked to his hands. "Let's talk about something else. I want to enjoy the evening and not have nightmares later because I dredged all of this up tonight."

"But he's the reason you're here? In Atlanta I mean. Is there something here that will help you learn more about him?"

Matt shook his head.

"Then what?"

"He's here."

"He's where?" Jane couldn't mask the excitement and rage in her question. "Atlanta?"

Matt nodded but didn't look up. "I don't know why I'm telling you this," he said with a sigh. "I tracked him through Iraq with a group of Marines. Now he's here in the States."

"How do you know?"

"What part of, *I don't want to discuss this* did you miss?" He laughed, trying to take the edge off his pointed question.

Jane stared with unblinking focus, catching his gaze and holding on for dear life.

Matt leaned into the table and brought his voice down. "I've been tracking him for about a year. He has a trail that's not too hard to follow—*if* you know where to look."

Jane wanted to call bullshit. Three left no trail. If he had, she would've found him and eliminated him herself. "So where are you looking?"

Matt leaned away and shook his head. "I'm not having this conversation."

Jane sat back. She knew she was going to have to get into Matt Matthew's pants before she could get into his head. If it meant finding Three, she didn't mind. It was two for the price of one.

Jane took his hand and gave it a squeeze. "I'm sorry. It was insensitive of me to push you like that. I understand—well, I mean, I *don't*. I don't know how you did it. Being out in the desert all that time. And now you're hunting for this bad guy. It's all so—"

Matt ran his fingers across Jane's. "Stupid?"

Jane pretended to be coy and looked to her lap before bringing her eyes to meet his. "Sexy."

Matt smiled and when a full-on blush covered his cheeks, Jane knew she had him. "You wanna get out of here?" she asked.

"Where do you wanna go?"

Jane raised one eyebrow. "You've seen my

place. How about you show me yours."

Matt leaned back in his chair and held up one finger to Perky Tits. "Check please."

DAY FOUR | 2300 HOURS

JANE LOOKED AROUND the apartment, noting her exit points—the front door and one window that dropped below to an in-ground pool and hot tub. Matt pulled two glasses from a cabinet over the bar in the eat-in kitchen and opened the freezer, taking out a bottle of dark rum before rummaging in the refrigerator for a can of ginger beer.

The apartment was a furnished deal. The furniture was black and easy to wipe down, the floors and carpets dark. It wasn't the *Island of Misfit Toys* like Beverly Court, but more of a sleek and modern short-term man cave. Only businessmen on extended trips with high priced hookers stayed in places like this. Jane wondered what that said about Matt.

"Can I fix you a Dark 'N Stormy?"

Jane shook her head.

Matt pointed her way, the rum still in his grip. "If you won't have a Dark 'N Stormy, how about a partly cloudy?" He laughed at his own joke and wiped the smile from his face when Jane didn't. "That's right. You don't drink. What if I said you had to at least have a little nightcap? My apartment. My rules."

"I'd say, I'm a rule breaker."

He gave her a smirk. "Water?"

She nodded.

He mixed his own drink, the ice plinking into the crystal highball glass one cube at a time. "Why, Scarlett?"

"Why what?"

Matt opened the black refrigerator, exchanging half a can of ginger beer for a bottle of water before shutting it with his hip. "No alcohol."

Jane blinked deliberately, but stood by the door, still carrying her backpack on her shoulder. "Dulls the senses."

Matt nodded toward the black leather couch, silently asking Jane to take a seat. She obliged him and he joined her. He sat close, but not uncomfortably so.

"But isn't that why everyone drinks in the

first place? To dull their senses. To *not* think?"

Jane didn't reply.

"I thought I knew how to party from my college days, but I truly learned how to drink—I mean *really* hold my liquor—while reporting in the Middle East. I did it *specifically* to dull my senses. We *all* did."

"I'm sure." And she was. She understood what Matt was referring to. She just never had the luxury of alcohol while deployed. When she did have time off, or some kind of entertainment was brought to the base, the last thing she wanted was to get plastered. She wanted to get laid, and she wanted to have her wits about her to at least enjoy it. Food, water, sex and survival. There was no room for alcohol.

Jane found it interesting Matt understood the life she'd lived, even if he wasn't aware of it. It was as if he knew her well and yet she'd not told him one specific detail of her life.

"This is the point in the evening when any self-respecting man would put on some music and make a move."

"And?"

"Sadly, I don't have any music in this place," he sighed, looking around the dark and modern apartment. "I don't even have music on my phone. But if *you* do, I can plug it into the clock radio. It has a docking station."

Jane shook her head.

"You don't have music on your phone either? Wow, we're even more alike than I thought."

"No. I don't have a phone."

His brows snapped together in disbelief. "What do you mean, you don't have a phone? I saw you using it when you were running."

Jane shook her head. "That was an old iPod. And before you ask, I *don't* have it in my bag."

Matt gave Jane the once-over from head to toe as she sat next to him and for the first time in as long as she could remember, she felt exposed. "What?" she asked.

He knitted his brow and took another sip of his drink before sitting it on the glass coffee table. He leaned back, bringing his two fingers to rest on his lips and the wheels in his head turned. Jane found it incredibly hot. "I dunno. *Something.*"

"What's that supposed to mean?" An edge of contempt laced her words.

"Don't get defensive." His deep voice turned into a low hum. "Let's just say I'm really good at watching and observing and I think there's more to you than what I see on the surface." Matt leaned into her and brushed a stray hair from Jane's face. His warm fingers grazed the side of her flushed cheek and she felt it through her entire body. Jane didn't touch people. She had sex, but she didn't touch—not in *that* way. Jane had boundaries. When they were truly broken, it affected her in ways she couldn't understand. There was an emotional bridge she didn't cross, something she'd shut down long ago—long before Matt Matthews stumbled into her cart at the library.

"I'm an onion. I guess."

One corner of his mouth lifted in an inquisitive smirk and he took Jane's hand in his own, giving it a squeeze. "I plan to peel back those layers, Scarlett Jenkins."

Matt leaned in, closing the space between their faces, silently inviting Jane to go the last millimeter to meet his eager mouth. Taking her time, she narrowed the small gap between them, stopping a breath from his lips to whisper. "I'm not really into kissing."

"You should be kissed, and often and by someone who knows how."

She balked, pulling away from the nearness of his mouth. He ran his hand up the nape of her long neck, pulling her back in. "What *are* you into?" His sweet breath washed across her lips.

"Sex."

He raised one eyebrow, but didn't flinch and moved a mere sigh from her lips. "Believe me, I've thought of making love to you from the moment I watched you running—that tight—" Matt hesitated and chose his words carefully. "*Body* and those sexy legs? Then I met you and on top of it all, you're so damn smart. I could be in real trouble here, Scarlett. I'm gonna need to take this one step at a time."

Jane closed her eyes and tilted her head back, wanting him to make the first step—a kiss. He didn't disappoint. His warm, open mouth brushed against her lips and a deep-seated longing overcame Jane at once. Taking her face in his hands, he kissed her again. She lingered on the sweet warmth of his lips. Matt enclosed her in his embrace, settling her deeper into the leather couch. Regardless of what he'd confessed, it was clear to Jane. Matt wanted *more*. How much more, Jane was willing to explore his limits.

He moaned, awakening a pang of wanting she'd never known. She'd been horny. She'd been hot and bothered, but this was something different. This seemed deeper. Jane thought it might be that she felt like herself when she was with him—truly herself. Was it possible Matt Matthews was capable of understanding her, given his past? Perhaps it was merely the *unknown* of the handsome man that turned her on. She kissed him hard, parting his lips with her tongue. He pulled her body to his, placing his hands on either side of her shoulders, pressing into her small, but rock hard frame.

"Dear God, do you feel that?" he asked, coming up for air.

Jane moved her hand from his shoulder to his crotch, lightly skimming the top of his pressed khakis. She'd never been a woman to shy away from what she wanted. "Yes."

"No," he chided. "Well, I mean, *of course* I can feel *that* and now that *you've* felt it, I can feel it even more. That's not what I'm talking about."

Jane kissed him again, her voice breathy in the heat of the moment. "Maybe you shouldn't talk." It was a guy's line. It was a *shut up and fuck me* line.

He kissed his way down her neck, pausing only to pull the yellow sweater and bra strap from her shoulder for better access. "Scarlett, as much as I'd love to pick you up and carry you to my bed right this moment, I won't. I won't do it. Not tonight."

She pulled away from him, her face blank with shock. "What?"

Matt sat back and adjusted the hard on in his pants. "Look, Scarlett. I care for you. I *really* care for you. I don't want this to be a one-night stand kinda thing. I have too much respect for you. I like you. I mean, I *really* like you. And I think you like me. Right?"

Jane stood abruptly, hanging her hands from her hips in exasperation. "Are you *kidding* me right now?"

Matt silenced his own shock with a guffaw. "No."

Jane dropped her head back, fueled by lust and sexual frustration. "Sweet Jesus. Why can't you be like other men and just screw me?"

Matt was clearly taken aback.

"Are you gay?"

Matt blanched. "No."

"Do you have some sort of disease I need to be aware of?"

"No."

"Do you find me repulsive?"

"*God, no.*"

Jane dropped her hands to her side. "Then what is it?"

Matt shook his head and bit his lip. He couldn't even look her in the eye. "I'm not that kind of guy."

"Are you serious? *Really?*"

"Look. I *am* that kind of guy. But if I just wanted to knock off a piece of ass, I would've picked up Perky Tits and brought her home, banged her into my headboard and sent her on her way in a taxi. That's not what I want. I mean, *it is*. Shit. This is *not* coming out right."

"You can say that again."

"I *do* want to be with you. I can't put it into words. Not really."

"Try." Jane was frustrated, her body eager, her mind racing with thoughts of the sexual release she desperately needed.

Matt hung his head and looked to his feet as he spoke. "I want to…" he hesitated then looked her in the eye. "I want to make *love* to you."

Jane knitted her brow and shook her head, silently questioning his remark.

"I know, I know. It's surprising the hell out of me too. It's just *something*. I don't know what, but there's something about you, Scarlett."

Jane let out a heavy sigh. "Fine." She was hot and horny. She was primed for the taking. She even had a couple of condoms in her backpack just in case Matt wasn't prepared. Now she was going home revved up with no one to screw *or* kill.

"I'm going," she said, picking up her backpack and slinging it over her shoulder.

Matt immediately came to his feet. "Don't go. You shouldn't go."

"No, I really *should*."

"Jesus," he sighed. "I feel like a complete ass. Let me drive you home."

Jane rolled her eyes again. "Fine."

"I need to ah…the alcohol and excitement—I have to pee."

"*Fine*," she droned again, glancing at the

bulge in his pants. She thought it a crying shame she'd wouldn't get to put it to good use.

"Be right back."

He disappeared into the bedroom. Flipping on the light, he illuminated the dark space for a split second. Something caught Jane's eye and she walked to the doorway for closer inspection.

Turning on the lamp next to the bed, she saw his open closet door. On the inside was a map of Atlanta, two photos of Three, an email addressed to Matt from Three himself and an Atlanta address. Jane memorized it, making mental notes of the red pins stuck in locations on the map.

The toilet flushed in the bathroom and Jane turned out the light, leaving the door ajar, hurrying into the other room. She opened the front door to his apartment and left without making a sound. A flickering bulb in the hallway was ready to blow and it lit her way to the stairs. She needed the fastest getaway.

Matt wasn't lying. He *was* on the trail of Three. But Jane didn't understand. If Three was in the same city with Thirteen, why in the hell wasn't she given directives to end them both?

Three's fingerprints were all over the planning of the coordinated attacks. So why was she sent to end *only* the life of Thirteen? And how in the *hell* did Matt Matthews get so close to Three in the first place?

DAY FIVE | ZERO DARK HUNDRED

MATT STARED AT his reflection in the mirror over the toilet and relieved himself. He thought it an odd place for the decorators of the furnished apartments to put a mirror—at least for a man. Watching himself pee wasn't something he liked particularly, but tonight it gave him a chance to fix his hair where it was standing straight up from his make-out session. Her hands had been all over him and he was as turned on as he could remember. At the same time, he felt bad for not granting her wish and sleeping with her. Matt knew if he could just hang on for a few more dates, he could get to know the woman who beguiled him with her wisdom, wit and no nonsense approach to life. She was the kind of woman who was adventurous—just like him. Someone who would take to the open road with him, leaving so many of the possessions most people valued behind. At least with the future he knew was probably ahead of him, that was his hope.

Matt flushed the toilet and washed his hands, running damp fingers across his dark waves one last time.

"Scarlett?" he called as he opened the door. "I was thinking, if you aren't volunteering tomorrow, we could head over to the Stone Mountain area. Maybe do some—"

Matt stood in the empty room. "Scarlett?"

He walked back into his bedroom, hitting the light switch. It was empty. "Scarlett?"

Baffled, Matt left the light on in his bedroom and walked back into the den a second time as if he would find something different— as if he'd find her sitting on the couch, waiting patiently for him. She wasn't. She was gone.

"What the hell?" He muttered the question under his breath and rushed to the front door, looking down the hallway both ways. There was no sign of her. It was as if she'd vanished into thin air.

He shouted her name down the hall and another resident shouted back. "Pipe down, shithead!"

Forgoing the elevator, Matt took to the staircase, hopping over the railing to the next flight at every turn. Bursting through the side door, he rushed into the parking lot shouting her name. "Scarlett? Where are you?"

The silence that surrounded him in the night was deafening. There was nothing. And there was no Scarlett.

Matt hung his hands on his hips in frustration. He couldn't call her. She didn't have a phone. The only thing he could do was drive to her apartment—make sure she made it home safely.

Tapping the keys in his pocket he hurried to his car, thinking he could catch her. She couldn't have gone far. Hopping inside, he turned the ignition as his phone rang out. He flinched.

The call was unknown, and for a moment Matt thought perhaps it was Scarlett calling from a payphone with an explanation. "Matthews."

The pause on the line made Matt's stomach

drop. He wasn't in the mood for another call from his father.

"Matthew?"

Matt turned off the car. "Yes?"

"Son, it's Collie."

"Collie?" Matt couldn't hide the surprise in his voice. General James P. Collins was a former Director of the CIA and Matt's godfather. Best friend to C. Matthew Matthews, he was the real reason Maxtronix was the billion-dollar company it was. It was Collie who pushed through the defense contracts decades ago—something that continued to extend and reinvent itself each time it came up for renewal. General Collins, like Matt's grandfather, was a man's man. Honest, hardworking, faithful to his family and his country. He was nothing like the man who now ran Maxtronix. Neither was Matt.

"Look Matt, I don't want to talk long. These phone lines have too many ears."

"Are you calling me from the Pentagon?"

"At midnight? Hell no. A payphone in front of the Pizza Hut a few blocks away. But I'm sure it's bugged all the same. Listen to me son. You need to get out."

"We've discussed this. I will. When it's done. When *I'm* done."

"Someone's been snooping around. Someone with a damned login and password. You know what that means, don't you?"

"Someone on the inside."

"You're gee-dee right, mister. Now I know you have things you need to prove, but you can't keep this up much longer. When it all unravels—and it will—

Matt cut him off. "I understand, sir. I do."

"Fine."

"How do you want me to get in touch with you?" Matt asked. "I'm going to need at least a couple more weeks. How will I find you?"

"You won't. I'll find you. Keep your head on a swivel, kiddo. I can only do so much inside the five-sided-squirrel cage."

"I understand, Collie. And thank you. For everything."

"I love ya like you're my own but I'll tell ya something, get it together, or I'm pulling the plug on you."

"You have my word."

DAY FIVE | ZERO DARK THIRTY

FUELED BY THE knowledge that Matt knew more about Three's whereabouts and her sexual frustration, Jane hopped a cab to the warehouse in Five Points. If the boys of the caliphate were home, she'd wait in one of the nearby alleyways for them to leave. If they were still grabbing ass at the strip club, she was going back inside for a closer look. She needed answers. Now.

Jane paid the driver, tipping him heavily, then stood on the street corner in the darkness of the night. She watched. She waited.

There was no van or truck in the loading dock. There were no lights. After casing the place for over twenty minutes, Jane crossed the street and prayed her cardboard key was still lodged in the door frame. It was her only way in, unless she planned on breaking and not just entering.

Jane paused in the shadows while a dump truck noisily rolled through the neighborhood. Once behind the building, she pressed her fingers into the crack around the metal door, prying it open.

The door gave way, and Jane opened it just enough to slip through sideways. She pulled the Maglite from the side pocket of her bag and began her search of the building. She'd prepared herself for the rats this time and wouldn't be caught off guard. Her sexual frustration gave her reason enough to kill the little bastards.

She walked to the tables in the middle of the warehouse. The papers, once gone, were back. She shuffled through each of them, mindful of their placement. She needed to confirm the date they planned to execute their attack. If they moved it up, Jane would be forced to simply shoot Thirteen. It would be messy. There would be retaliation. She would be hung out to dry, but lives would be saved.

A calendar covered in cows from a chicken

place in Atlanta sat alone at the end of the first table. The fourth Thursday in April was circled. Jane suspected there was a significance to the day. What it was, she wasn't sure.

There were invoices for a custom vehicle decal. A food truck—*Big Mama's Burger Wagen*. Jane raised one eyebrow. They'd spelled *Wagon* wrong. Still, it was how they planned to move past any security that could impede their trek into the center of the park. She examined the plans for the two buildings again and sorted through the papers looking for any new communication directives from Three. She found nothing.

She worked her way through the building, locating the acetone again in the same spot. There was no peroxide—not yet. To Jane it was a sign that the person who was making the bombs knew of the volatility. They weren't bringing in a hack. They were making sure the mission was successful. With two of the most wanted terrorists on her list now involved in the same mission, it was clear they were pulling out all the stops. There would be no room for error on their part—which only made Jane's job more difficult.

She moved on to another table away from the plans. From a distance it looked like photographs—she hadn't noticed them or the table the first night she'd inspected the space with old man DeLuca.

Moving in closer, she found more propaganda in Arabic along with photos of women's bodies cut apart—their heads side by side. Their legs and arms lined up with their torsos— the body parts separated. It looked like a meat market from a twisted horror film. But it was all real. Every damn bit of it.

Under the photos of the women, was a note from Three himself. He'd even signed it in a known fashion, tracked by the FBI and U.S. military forces. SDK3. The sonofabitch mocked the men and women looking for his ass by adding the number three to his initials. He was well aware he was number three on the government's terror list. One and Two were already dead. Neither one by Jane's hand, but they were dead all the same.

Attached to his note which read, *Make an example of the infidel. Kill him for the world to see* was a dog-eared photograph.

"No." She gasped, saying the word aloud.

In her hand was a four by six photo of Matt Matthews—sunglasses on his head, cross-body bag over his shoulder, scarf around his neck. The photo looked as if it was taken in the desert, but it was hard to be certain. On the back was an address—not the one Jane had just come from, but another—in Pittsburgh.

Matt was on the verge of being shot or getting his head cut off. They planned to film and release it to the public. That was what Three meant—*for the world to see.* Nothing pleased him more than to film the death of those who did not believe as he did.

Jane had to warn Matt. Three's men would come looking for him. If anyone was at his home in Pittsburgh, they'd be tortured to give up his current location.

The problem now, was how to keep Matt safe without blowing her own cover. "Shit," she hissed under her breath. *"Cocksuckingmotherfuck-ingsonofabitch."*

DAY FIVE | 0500 HOURS

JANE DROVE THE Accord to Matt's apartment and parked near the exit of the four story building. An on-duty doorman stood behind the glass under the awning. Jane stayed out of sight. She waited.

At five-thirty, Jane spied Matt in her rear-view mirror. He'd been up earlier than she expected for his run. Maybe he was as frustrated over last night as she was. She climbed out of the car to meet him in her jeans, tank top and grey hoodie. She kept her car door open, leaning against the trunk—waiting.

The doorman walked outside as Matt slowed his pace to greet her.

He glistened from head to toe, his tight body on display. She shook her head at him, unable to keep her feelings under control. "I need you to get in."

He stared at her, his usual dark waves now in tight ringlets, wet with perspiration. "What happened to you last night? Do you know I drove to your apartment? Did you even go home?"

"Get in."

"Why?"

"Get. In."

"No. Tell me what's going on."

"Is there a problem, Mr. Matthews?" Matt's doorman came outside, his body parting the early morning fog. By the sheer size of him, he looked like a comic book hero coming on the scene through the mist. Jane feared he'd want to act like a hero, too. She let out a heavy sigh. It was turning into a shit show of a day and the sun wasn't even up.

"No Dan," Matt replied, holding his hand in the air. "I'm fine."

Jane didn't look the doorman in the face. The last thing she wanted was to be identified later. She stared at Matt and didn't blink. "Get in the car."

"Why?"

She looked to their feet. She was two steps from Matt—the doorman three steps behind her. "Don't make me do this."

"Do what?"

"I'll ask you nicely one more time. Get in the car."

"Nicely is saying the word, please. I didn't hear the word, *please*," he said, wiping the sweat from his brow with the tail of his shirt.

"Please."

"Not unless you tell me what's going on and why you left last night."

She took a deep breath. The doorman moved his foot a fraction of an inch, and as Jane exhaled she turned and made Danny the Doorman's morning very upsetting indeed.

Pretending to pull a gun, Jane waited for Dan to flinch. Reaching for his pepper spray, he sat into a shooters stance—painting a target on his groin. One blow from her knee, and he fell like a drunk girl in heels at a frat house kegger—awkward as ass. He struggled to get to his feet. Jane said one word, "Sorry" before dealing the final blow to his temple via her elbow. It was lights out for Danny Boy.

Matt stood back in shock. "Whoa! What the hell just happened?"

Jane took him by the arm and led him to

the passenger side of the car. "Give me the keys to your apartment."

"Why?"

"Because we can't come back here and you can't go upstairs. You're a liability. Give me the keys. Sit here in the car and be quiet. Dan will be asleep for at least thirty minutes."

"Jesus Christ." Matt pulled the lone key from the waistband of his running shorts. "I don't know who you are or what the hell you're involved with, but you're not going anywhere near my apartment without me."

"Fine," Jane replied. "But if there's trouble upstairs, this time for God's sake, follow orders. Got it?"

Jane took him by the arm and hustled him into the building. Matt walked to the elevator. Jane whistled. "Yo. This way." She opened the door to the stairwell and waited for him to begin the climb. "Stay quiet."

"Tell me what in the hell you're up to? What's going on?" Matt's patience was openly thin.

Jane said nothing. When they reached the fourth floor, she held him off, opening the door to peer down the hallway. "Okay," she said, waving him forward. "You need to be quick."

"Yeah," Matt said as he slid the key into the lock. "You said that."

"And quiet," she whispered.

Shutting the door behind them, Jane strode to the bedroom, ripping open the closet door to remove every item taped inside it.

Matt stuttered. "Hey! What the fuck? I need that! How did you—?"

"I saw it last night. Look, he knows you're in town. *He's tracking you*. If you want to stay alive you'll listen to me and do everything I say."

"Who *are* you? Who are you with?"

"Get your bag, get a change of clothes. If you have any items of sentimental value take them with you. You're not coming back."

"Can I shower?"

Jane paused and her face screwed into a tight expression of *whatthafuck?* "Get your shit together, Matthews. Literally *and* figuratively."

"I was kidding."

"Now? You're picking *this* moment to crack a joke?" she asked, folding the map from the closet door into a smaller square and tucking it into her back pocket along with the other items.

"Let's go."

He nodded and followed her out the door, locking it behind him. Rushing down the stairwell again, they made it down one flight when Jane turned to Matt and placed a single finger across her lips. She froze in her tracks. Two men were speaking in Arabic.

"Are you sure this is the building?"

"Yes. It's the correct plate on the car."

Jane grabbed him by the arm, tugging him up the staircase by his shirt. Matt did his best to lean over and look at the men making their way up the stairwell.

Climbing another flight higher, Jane waited on the fifth floor, keeping Matt close to her. She listened until the door one flight down closed. Jane pulled Matt out of the stairwell by the hand. "Elevator."

"Now?"

The doors opened and she pushed him into the lift, pressing the lobby button over and over in rapid succession.

"You know that doesn't make it go any faster."

Jane said nothing, but stared into his ruddy and sweating face as the elevator descended and

Barry Manilow sang softly in the background of ships passing in the night.

"You know he wrote a ton of jingles," Matt said pointing up to the speaker.

Jane said nothing. She watched numbers overhead as they descended, shaking her head at his comment.

"Sorry. It's just—I say stupid shit when I'm nervous."

The bell rang out and the doors opened. They needed to hurry. If Tweedle A and Tweedle B had been sent for Matt as Jane suspected, they'd sweep the parking lot and find the unconscious doorman. She needed to hide him—fast.

"I need you to stay calm. We need to hide Dan."

"Where?"

They rushed through the front door to where he still lay on the pavement. Jane grabbed his shoulders, Matt his feet. "Behind the building. He'll be awake soon, calling the cops I'm sure."

Matt calmly shook his head. "No, he won't. He supplies half the building with coke and amphetamines. He won't call anyone."

Jane propped his head against a bag of landscape cedar chips, hiding his body behind a row of bushes.

They stopped at the side of the building, Jane peering around the corner to make sure the coast was clear.

She motioned for Matt to follow her and pointed to the Honda Accord.

They sped away, the exhaust twisting in a corkscrew as the sun peeked over the horizon.

Matt took a breath. "Where are we going?"

"My place," she said making a turn on a yellow light, causing oncoming cars to slam on brakes, honk horns and throw up middle fingers.

"For someone who doesn't want to be seen, you're sure stirring up a shit storm."

Jane didn't look at him. She concentrated on the road and ran every scenario through her head where the plan to stop Thirteen worked out. She couldn't find one. Saving Matt was going to screw up her mission. It was going to screw up her life.

"Wanna tell me who you *really* are?" Matt's obvious fear had turned to sarcasm.

Jane was terse in her reply. "No."

"Well, what the fuck anyway?"

"Tell me why you're tracking SDK3."

"SDK- *three?*" Matt's voice rose and he furrowed his brow.

"Fine. SDK."

"I've—" Matt hesitated. "I've been in contact with him for a story. For some reason he trusts me. He agreed to an interview."

"Why in the hell would you want to interview *him?* What purpose would it serve?" Jane pulled into the parking lot of Beverly Court and killed the engine but didn't get out of the car.

"I *told* him I'd give his point of view. What he wants Westerners to know about their movement. *I* want to know who he's working with."

Jane smirked, rolled her eyes and climbed from the car, slamming the door.

"What?" Matt hustled out, following her closely. "Is there some crime in interviewing him? And why do you care anyway? What are you? FBI? CIA?"

Jane climbed the steps to her apartment two by two, opened the door and waited for Matt to walk in. Frustration was painted across her face. "No."

Matt crossed the threshold into Jane's apartment, dropping his bag on the closest plaid chair. "What then? Why are you pushing me around? Making me leave my apartment? Why would you ever think those men were coming for me?"

Jane placed the key to her apartment on the kitchenette and walked into her bedroom without answering him. She needed to get dressed for the library, and the outfit she'd chosen for the day now had a splatter of the doorman's blood on it. She'd have to wear the yellow sweater again.

"Are you going to answer me?"

Jane stuck her head out of the bedroom in only her bra and jeans and pulled the sweater, still buttoned up from the night before over her head. She fashioned her hair into a sleek ponytail using only her fingers.

"Scarlett?"

"What?" She turned on her heel, tired of questions. She needed Matt to stay put. She needed him to keep out of sight. It was the only way she could protect him. After the morning's activities it was clear to Jane he couldn't protect himself. She didn't fault him. No one was typically prepared for jihadis to come knocking on the door like she was. He'd be safe in her apartment.

"Tell me what's going on, or I'm walking out this door."

Jane raised one eyebrow and shook her head. "Is this all an act? Or do you really not have a clue, Matt?" She moved into him. "If you walk out that door, you're as good as dead. Take my advice, stay inside this apartment until I return. You'll be safe here." Jane picked up her backpack and opened it, making sure her gun was locked and loaded and more importantly, right where she wanted it.

She hurried back to the bathroom, dug through the medicine cabinet taking what she required for the job and every syringe she had. She needed to be prepared for anything. *Everything.*

Matt stood at the foot of her unmade bed, hanging his hands on his hips—annoyed. "You can't leave me here not knowing where in the hell you're going."

Jane walked past him, brushing his shoulder and knocking him back a step. She opened the front door. "Of course I can. And Matt?"

"What?"

"Take a shower. You smell."

JANE GUNNED THE engine and tore out of the parking lot in the Accord. She needed to get to the library so she could make contact with Crow. Was it possible Washington was unaware she could take out Thirteen *and* Three? It wouldn't be the first time the suits were behind in their intel. The people in the trenches knew more about the targets, their habits and whereabouts than the desk jockeys. Still, she washed the idea of killing them both from her mind as quickly as it had appeared.

Jane pulled into the parking lot, hoping none of the other employees had arrived yet. She didn't want to be seen driving the boss's car. The lot was empty and she parked in Sam's usual spot.

Using his keys, Jane let herself into the library, dead-bolting the door behind her. It would be at least two hours before anyone showed up to work or volunteer. It was the two hours Jane needed to get online and do some digging.

She logged into the system as an eighty-five-year old male patron of the library via his e-library card. She had a To Do list in her head: contact Crow, find out the significance of the fourth Tuesday in April and figure out what to do with Matt Matthews when the mission was complete.

Pulling up a social media webpage, she found Crow's fake identity. It was filled with surfing videos, rants about his favorite sports teams, the occasional meme and lots of ways to incorporate kale into your diet. She found his latest post: Thirty Favorable Traits in a Partner. It was a list of items someone deemed important for a healthy relationship. She replied using her own fake identity—a forty-something woman who wasn't married, owned a slew of cats and posted casserole recipes on her wall.

I'd like 13 and 3. Is it possible to have both of those in only one man?

She posted the comment and waited, keeping the window open while she logged into the NSA mainframe. She was only to use the database to search for information on her targets. She'd have to explain her reasoning to

Crow when it came back to bite her in the butt—and it would.

Once in, she typed in his name, three ways: Matt Matthews, C. Matthew Matthews and Christopher Matthew Matthews III.

She had a hit on two names. Christopher Matthew Matthews, deceased. Christopher Matthew Matthews, II aged sixty-two. There was no record for number three. It simply wasn't possible. Jane put his name in again, leaving off the Christopher and opting only for Matt Matthews. Bingo. He wasn't tied to the first two and more than that, his records were classified. She tried again to access the information. As a member of the small group in the Coywolf Project, Jane was TS/SCI or top secret sensitive compartmented information eligible. She had access to information at the highest level. Again, she was denied.

"Who *are* you, Matt Matthews?"

Running out of time, Jane did a simple Google search. *What is the significance of the fourth Thursday of April?*

Google churned, sending her a page of blue hyperlinks. The top link told her everything she needed to know. She read the words aloud in a hollow voice. "Take Our Daughters and Sons to Work Day."

Jane sat back in the chair. Three's plan, executed by her target, Thirteen, was to detonate three TATP bombs in downtown Atlanta during the morning rush hour while thousands of mothers and fathers walked hand in hand with their children into the work place. It was the worst scenario she could think of. And it was going to play out in front of her very eyes if she didn't stop it.

MATT SHOWERED IN Jane's apartment, using a towel that was still slightly damp to dry off. He left the clean one hanging on the bar over the toilet. He didn't mind. He liked the way the towel smelled—like her. Naked, he walked into the main room of the apartment and opened his satchel, searching for pants and a shirt. He knew he'd thrown clothes into the bag, but wasn't exactly sure what he'd grabbed. It didn't take long to realize he hadn't packed underwear.

Pulling his jeans on commando, he fought

his way into the arm holes of his t-shirt, slopping it over his head.

He took only a beat and thought of his conversation the night before with Collie. Was Scarlett the person digging into his files? She certainly acted like covert ops. She was bossy enough for the job too. She didn't learn how to fight like that in a self-defense seminar. She'd been trained. And trained well. Barefoot, he made his way back into Jane's bathroom, looking for antiperspirant. If his day was going to end the way it started, he would need it.

Matt opened the medicine cabinet praying she didn't use some girly deodorant that would make him smell flowery and found vials of liquid medication. One by one, he examined them, reading their names out loud, as if it would help him understand what they were used for. "Quelicin. M99. M5050. Ketalar." He sounded them out one by one, only familiar with the final vial. It was ketamine—an anesthetic. "Who *are* you? *What* are you?"

Matt examined each vial closely before closing the mirrored cabinet, forgetting he was looking for deodorant. Pacing the apartment, he picked up the only shoes he had—Nikes—and the sweaty socks still on the floor of Jane's bathroom. He sat on the edge of her bed and put them back on, the clammy dampness of the socks and shoes now cold from the air conditioner running full blast in the window.

He was famished, thirsty and not just for water or food. He was hungry for knowledge. He needed to know what was going on, and he needed to know now. Opening the olive green fridge, he found a couple of water bottles, an apple and another vial. Humalog. Matt wondered if she was diabetic and thought back to their dinner where she drank regular sodas.

"I swear woman, if you screw up my plans because you're some rogue agent carrying out God only knows what mission, I'll have to kill you. That is, unless Collie gets to me first."

He opened a bottle of water and chugged it, still parched from all the excitement. Matt surveyed the room looking for something—anything. Laying on the yellowed kitchen dinette was everything she'd pulled from his closet wall. He sat, sorting through it. He noted the locations he knew SDK to be in the city. He had a phone number stored in his cell—he could pick up the phone and call him—that was if SDK hadn't changed phones—which he'd been known to do. The last thing he wanted was for two years of planning to go down the toilet. He had no reason to believe SDK was *looking* for him. Now suddenly a crazy chick who would barely speak to him had his balls in her purse along with his plan. Years of preparation was circling the drain. Matt shook his head. He wasn't going to allow it to happen. Between being blown off last night and bossed around this morning, Matt made a decision. She wasn't stopping him from accomplishing what he'd come to Atlanta to do.

He gathered up the papers she'd so carelessly ripped from his closet and neatly stacked them in a pile. He rearranged the few things he'd thrown into his bag, taking out his sweaty shorts and shirt and the shemagh he wore nearly every day. He slid his stack of gathered intel into the bag, leaving the running clothes and scarf behind.

He didn't have a car, but he still had his key and he could walk back to his own apartment. From there it was a ride to the last known location Matt knew SDK to be.

As he closed the door to her apartment, he whispered the words. "Sorry, Scarlett."

DAY FIVE | 0845 HOURS

J ANE LOCKED HERSELF in Drunk Sam's office. The library would open soon and others would be arriving. She had too much to do and couldn't be bothered with questions. No one knew she was even in the building. She made a mental checklist in her head. She needed to track A and B. She needed to track Thirteen. She *wanted* to track Three. If she was unsuccessful in terminating Thirteen, she needed to find a way to stop the attack in four days—even if it meant outing herself. It was the best planned, most diabolical, coordinated event she'd seen to date. And it scared the shit out of her.

She sat down at Sam's desk again and Googled the name of the person in charge at Georgia Natural Gas. Bingo. Gary Tinker. She memorized his phone number. Jane then used the NSA database to search for Tinker's cell phone number. She'd already have to answer for her inquiry into Matt Matthews. She would get called on the carpet for both moves, but desperate times called for desperate measures. With limited resources, she had to do what she could. Jane thought through her plan one last time, then checked her fake social media account and found a response from Crow. His reply was one number. *Thirteen.*

"Shit." She mumbled the word under her breath. She was only authorized to eliminate her initial target. *Not* Three. Jane shook her head and closed her eyes. If she lived through the next twenty-four hours she was going to have words for Crow. She already knew he would have words for her. In the meantime, she needed to do her best to stay alive and execute her mission. Kill Thirteen.

Jane closed out the windows on Sam's computer, turned out the lights and shut the door behind her. She passed Doe Eyes in the break room as she took the back exit to the parking lot. Jane was thankful she didn't have to engage in conversation.

She started Sam's car. She needed gas and

she needed to make a quick trip to Walmart for supplies. If her plan to stop Thirteen was going to work she needed zip ties and pillowcases.

She made the turn, driving past the warehouse. There were no vans, no cars. Making a U-turn in the middle of the empty street, she parked directly in front of DeLuca's and killed the engine. She stared at the old building and fought the urge to enter it again.

Three loud raps rang out inside the car. Jane turned to find Mr. DeLuca banging on her passenger's window. Unruffled, she got out and joined him on the sidewalk. It was beginning to drizzle as dark clouds rolled in, blocking out the sun.

"What are you doing here?" He looked from her to the warehouse across the street and back to her.

Jane shrugged.

"You still interested in the building, si?"

Jane nodded.

"Come with me." The old man ushered Jane out of the rain and into the dark pizza parlor, locking the door behind them.

"You hungry?"

Jane popped her eyebrows. She was. And

Jane was rarely hungry. She nodded.

DeLuca waved his hand for her to follow him into the kitchen. "Come."

Jane walked through the empty tables. The smell of clean floors and ammonia from the previous nights' cleaning still lingered in the air. DeLuca directed her into the stainless steel kitchen—the lights shining on the clean equipment. It was clear to Jane, DeLuca took pride in his business. "Why the warehouse?" He pointed across the street, their view now blocked by a wall.

Jane shrugged.

"I like you, Scarlett. You nice girl." DeLuca walked the kitchen, a path so familiar he didn't need to watch where he was going. He pulled a clean apron from a peg and placed it over his head. His arthritic hands were slow to tie the knot. DeLuca wagged his finger at Jane. "Something not right."

She narrowed her gaze. "What do you mean?"

DeLuca pointed to her. "Your name is not Scarlett. Si?" He made his accusation with clarity and certainty. Jane looked to her feet and back to him. She felt exposed, and yet, safe in the company of the old man.

"It's the eyes. The name is not in your eyes."

Jane said nothing.

"It is said that when a baby is born, the mother and father don't choose name—it is whispered to them by God." DeLuca pointed and even looked to the heavens. "He knows your name. Even before you born." He preached passionately from his imaginary pulpit.

Jane shrugged it off. No one had whispered anything into anyone's ear upon her birth. They'd just left her in a dumpster, cold, hungry, and waiting to die.

DeLuca opened a pizza oven and the smell of fresh bread filled the kitchen. Shoving a flat peel inside, he retrieved four small loaves of bread, tossing them onto a wooden board to cool.

DeLuca walked to the coffee machine, pulling a white mug from under the counter. "Cappuccino?"

Jane shook her head. "I don't drink coffee."

DeLuca shrugged, turning his mouth upside down in disapproval. "Eh. Water?"

"I really don't have—" Jane hesitated. "I don't have time."

Picking a clean glass out of a rack, he stopped at the large refrigerator for a pitcher of water, placing it all on the steel prep table in the center of the kitchen.

He nodded. "Sit. You eat. *Then* you go."

Jane did as she was told. She sat on one of the two stools and watched DeLuca slice and butter a piece of warm bread for her. It was the nicest thing she could remember anyone doing for her in a very long time. When she reflected on that moment, she felt sad. Pathetic. She took a bite, savoring the warmth of the bread and the saltiness of the melting butter. She closed her eyes. "Mmmm."

When she opened them, DeLuca was smiling. Nodding. He said, "Why the warehouse?"

Jane took a deep breath. "I don't like the people you're leasing it to."

"That makes two of us!" He dropped his hand to the table, causing a clang that rang out across the tile floor. "I call. I call the tip line."

Jane sat the bread on the counter. "Wait. You *called* a tip line?"

"Si." DeLuca nodded and pointed across the street again. "I think they up to no good."

Jane nodded. She knew they were up to no good. "Mr. DeLuca, you said something the other day. You said you'd be better off if the warehouse burned to the ground."

"Si, but no."

"Yes but no?"

DeLuca nodded.

"Are you saying you'd like for it to burn down, but you're not going to do anything illegal?"

"Il diavolo fa le pentole ma non i coperchi."

Jane didn't know enough Italian to make out the entire phrase, but she knew *diavolo*. "The devil does what?"

"Makes pots," he said picking up a large stock pot in one hand and the lid in the other. "Not lids."

"You don't want to do anything dishonest or illegal."

DeLuca nodded. "The truth always comes out."

"Do you have insurance on the warehouse? In case something happens?"

"Si. Milioni."

"A million dollars."

DeLuca nodded.

Jane stood. It was time to go. "Thank you for the bread, but I have…I have errands to run."

DeLuca took Jane's hands in his own. Rough, but warm, he gave her fingers a squeeze. He stared into her face. His aging eyes saw through her and she knew it. "Be well…Scarlett. Che Dio sia con te."

Jane smiled and repeated his words. "God be with me?"

He nodded.

She dropped his hands and looked away. It was time to go. Jane didn't do *feelings*. "Thank you again for…" she paused at the door of the kitchen. "Well…for everything."

Pushing the swinging door out, she took no time making tracks to the front door. She unlocked it and walked out, the bell chiming over her head. Jane didn't look back. She never looked back.

She stared across the street at the warehouse. The drizzle had stopped and the sun was breaking through the clouds. It was quiet. No cars. No vans.

She adjusted the backpack on her shoulders and crossed the street. Traffic was starting to pick up. She was taking a risk being seen in the middle of the day, but time was running out. She needed to get inside. Jane needed to set the stage before executing her plan.

Hurrying to the back door, she pulled at the crease, digging the tips of her fingers into the rusty metal to pry it open. With a loud creak, it gave way. Jane slipped inside and closed the door, making sure the cardboard was sticking out from the frame.

Sunlight from the windows high in the peak of the roof on the east side of the building streaked across the floor, lighting up the room. There was no need for a flashlight—no need for lights at all.

She opened her backpack, sliding a roll of duct tape onto her wrist like a bracelet. Tearing off four equal strips and sticking the end to the sleeve of her sweater, she wandered to the center of the space, measuring her steps equal distance from the exits in the room. An empty filing cabinet sat in a nearby corner three feet away from her desired point. Jane reached around between waist and shoulder height. It was a tight squeeze. She pulled the cabinet out two inches, then dug in her bag for a gun.

She locked and loaded the M1911—safety off—taping it to the backside of the cabinet. Turning, she surveyed the room and hurried to the utility closet, dropping a hammer behind the door.

Jane walked back to the tables in the main room. The acetone was still in the corner. She searched for the peroxide mixture and the remaining ingredients Thirteen would need. She found nothing. Still, Jane knew the plan was moving forward. The food truck had been delivered into the warehouse, the new decal now emblazoned on its side.

Jane walked the inside perimeter of the warehouse looking for something—anything. She needed a little help from the universe.

A window she'd never noticed sat on the west side of the building—blacked in with dark paint. Jane didn't know if she believed in God or not, still, she looked to the heavens just as DeLuca had. "Thank you," she whispered.

She hurried to the gallon jugs of acetone, taking one from the darkest shadow under the table. Rushing back to the window, she stacked three boxes on top of each other and climbed to the window ten feet above her, moving the gallon of acetone up each box as she went. Using the hand sanitizer in her pocket, she globbed it on the corner of the window and rubbed. A small patch of black came off in her fingers. She'd painted her target. Placing the flammable liquid in the far western edge of the blackened pane high above the tables below and out of sight, the silver can would be visible from outside the building only if you were looking for it.

Jane climbed down the boxes, jumping to the ground. As soon as her feet hit the concrete, the front door opened.

Standing face to face with Jane was none other than Thirteen himself. And he had a friend with him—Three.

DAY FIVE | 1000 HOURS

T TOOK MATT Matthews less time than he'd anticipated to return to his apartment. Hopping an Uber, he was back in less than twenty minutes, even in morning traffic.

He thanked the driver, shut the door and stood in front of his apartment building. A pang of anxiety overcame him. Perhaps he'd made a mistake in coming back. What if she was right? What if the men really *were* looking for him?

Matt took a deep breath, shook it off and opened the glass door. The main entrance was quiet—too quiet. Dan the doorman was nowhere to be found. Matt assumed he was sitting in the nearest ER waiting for someone to assess him for concussion.

He shook his head, thinking about the altercation and slammed the elevator button with his open palm. He didn't know if he was frustrated over Scarlett leaving him in the dark, or if he was simply pissed and highly emasculated. She'd kicked Dan's ass. Dan with the biceps. Six-four, two-forty Dan. Matt cursed himself for not hitting the gym each day as he passed the big lug on his way up to his apartment.

The elevator opened with a loud *ding* and he climbed aboard, punching the four with his fist. Matt took a deep breath. It was quiet with the exception of the heinous music playing in the background. It had never bothered him before—the cheesy selection for his ride up or down was usually a funny distraction—but after this morning, everything was under his skin—especially Scarlett Jenkins.

Straight to the fourth floor, he exited the elevator onto the darkened hallway—the flickering wall sconce that lit his way had finally burned out. "Shit." The whole scene was starting to hit him in the gut—the gut he'd learned to trust over the last two years. He shook it off, reminding himself he wasn't in Iraq, he was in Atlanta. "Stop being a pussy," he said aloud, taking deliberate strides toward his apartment door. He looked to the keys in his palm and suddenly realized he was locked out of his own apartment. The key he'd used to get in this morning was tucked in his running shorts—which were now laying in a sweaty heap in the middle of Scarlett's floor. "Shit." He placed his hand on the knob in frustration. The door opened with a gentle push.

"What tha…"

Matt took a step inside and closed the door behind him. The once pristine, fully furnished man cave of an apartment had been ripped apart. Every glass in the cabinet was shattered on the floor, every plate, every utensil thrown from the drawers. Every item in the kitchen was strewn across the white tile floor. The leather couch had been gutted. Matt ran his fingers along the cuts—whatever they used was sharper than anything they'd found in his kitchen.

"Guess I'm not getting my security deposit back." Stepping over pillows that had been turned inside out, he walked to the bedroom. It was the same deal. His clothes were out of the drawers and thrown across the room. His wallet had been raped and pillaged—no money, cards or drivers' license remained.

His closet was empty, the wall safe open

and bare. "Fuck me." he hissed. His passport, two thousand dollars in cash and press badge were gone. All gone. He didn't go into the bathroom—he already knew it looked the same as the rest of the apartment. He could smell his shower gel without stepping foot into the room.

Matt picked up as many clothes as he could and stuffed them into the suitcase they'd torn the lining from.

He sat on the bed and stared at the inside of the closet—the place where his entire scheme to meet and interview SDK had hung. Once full of his grand plan, the only thing left was a piece of tape. Everything was going to hell in a handbasket. His plan, his life—even Scarlett. Matt didn't know what to believe or more importantly, who to trust. Scarlett was no library volunteer. And she knew too much about SDK to be just an undercover cop. Scarlett was something else—and in more ways than one.

Pulling the handle up on the ragged luggage, Matt rolled through the apartment, kicking debris out of his path. From the corner of his eye, he spotted the bottle of dark rum on the kitchen counter that had somehow manage to survive the havoc wrought throughout the apartment.

He parked the suitcase, mindful of the broken glass. Matt grabbed the bottle by the neck and opened it immediately, taking a gulp. He exhaled and wiped his mouth before screwing the top back on. He decided no one could fault him for drinking at ten in the morning. Not on a day like today.

He tucked the bottle under his arm and dragged the ragtag suitcase out the door.

It was the last thing Matt would remember.

DAY FIVE | 1010 HOURS

J ANE STAYED CALM and stared into the eyes of the person she'd dreamt of killing nearly every night for the past four years. His complexion wasn't one of a man who'd been lost in the desert. Matt's face showed more signs of roughing it in the Middle East than Three. He was actually more fair skinned and blue eyed. But she knew this about him already. She just didn't expect him to be as visually appealing in person. Father Doheny always told her Satan himself was beautiful to behold. He, too, was once an angel.

It's what she felt she was in the presence of—evil. Evil dressed as a normal man. She barely noticed Thirteen standing next to him.

"Ah. Si, si, si!" DeLuca rushed past them both, hurrying to Jane's side. "She is the one looking to rent when you go. I let her in and go back to restaurant for a moment while she look around."

"What did I tell you, old man?" Thirteen clenched his teeth when he spoke. He was the easy type of evil—the kind anyone would instinctively stay away from. The kind you could spot at twenty paces. Thirteen was a man who'd overseen the killing of fifteen young girls because they refused to have sex with his soldiers. He peddled them, carting the girls around like cattle in cages on trucks. He was the worst kind of person—and still not as horrific as Three.

Jane's heart pounded. She immediately went into autopilot—survival mode, lowering her heart rate by breathing. She didn't move a muscle. She only stared.

"I told you no one was to be in here. No one!"

Thirteen shouted in DeLuca's face, spittle falling into his beard with each enunciation. DeLuca took it. He didn't even blink.

Jane took inventory of the situation. She was a few feet from a loaded semi-automatic weapon. She could go for it, mow them both down and walk away for good. She could pull the knife from the leg of her pants and slit both of their throats. They'd be dead before their bodies hit the ground.

Jane knew she couldn't do either of those things. Jane followed orders. And her orders were to eliminate Thirteen. Crow had been specific. Three was to be unharmed. Besides, she would never allow a witness to her kill. It wasn't her style. Jane had borne witness to enough tragedy in her life between the Marines and foster care. She would never let her actions become the reason an innocent soul such as DeLuca couldn't sleep at night.

"I'm sorry," Jane began. "I just got here. I was looking at the scaffolding," she said, pointing to the ceiling without taking her eyes off Three.

Both men looked up—exactly where Jane wanted them to. DeLuca caught her eye and blinked hard, closing his eyes and opening them again. He was afraid.

"Is it yours? Or will it be left behind when your lease is up?"

Thirteen laughed, showing his yellow teeth. Jane thought he looked like an ass—literally. She wondered how big his smile would be when she reminded him just before ending his life he would die at the hands of a woman. There would be no virgins, no martyrdom for Thirteen. Being killed by a woman meant one thing—he was doomed to burn in hell. If there was a hell.

DeLuca wiped the sweat from his brow. "It belong to an old tenant. They leave it behind."

Jane nodded and walked toward the men with confidence, stopping only when she was toe to toe with both of them. "Mr. DeLuca, I'm happy to take over the lease when your business with these men has concluded. I'll check back with you. In the meantime, do you mind showing me the other space? You know, the one across town?"

DeLuca dropped his shoulders, feeding off of the calm Jane projected. "Si. Of course."

Jane looked Thirteen in the face before turning her attention to Three. "Sorry again… *fellas*."

DeLuca didn't say goodbye. He backed out the front door and held it for Jane. She felt the eyes of Three and Thirteen on her as she walked away. It was their first meeting, but it wouldn't be their last.

DeLuca waited until they'd crossed the street before saying a word. Jane walked into the pizza parlor. She didn't want to drive away in the car until she knew they had both left the warehouse. She'd have a tail for sure.

DeLuca locked the door to the restaurant behind them. "Perché? Why? Why?"

"I can't tell you why. But thank you for saving me. You did good, Mr. DeLuca. You did real good."

The old man wiped the remaining beads of sweat from his forehead and sat in the nearest booth away from the window. Like Jane, he knew better than to be a clear target through the glass—especially now.

"When I was ten," DeLuca began. "My father taught me how to hide. How to stay small, go unnoticed." DeLuca unbuttoned his sleeve, rolling it up high enough for Jane to make out the six digits tattooed on his arm, then promptly rolled it down again. It wasn't a badge of honor for the elderly man, but a reminder of the kind of hate that was capable of existing in the world.

"You need to be careful. You need to stay safe."

Jane nodded. "I need to stay here until they leave. I can't," she began pointing to the Honda Accord parked on the street.

He nodded and stood in front of her. "Stay out of sight."

"I will."

"And when you leave, don't come back. They will kill my family, just for spite."

Jane nodded. "I understand."

Deluca went into the kitchen. Jane sat in a darkened corner. She had two options. She could steal DeLuca's car parked in the back, or wait out the boys in the warehouse.

The clock on the wall of the restaurant ticked away and with each halt of the second hand, Jane knew she was losing time—precious time.

Just as she slung her backpack over her shoulder, the food truck backed out of the loading dock area and down a ramp to the parking lot. Jane assumed they were making a dry run with the truck—casing the park for the optimal place to detonate.

She waited for the truck to pull away, spying both men in the front of the vehicle.

Wasting no time, she rushed out the door

passing Darren. It was perfect timing. She didn't need DeLuca to lock the door behind her.

A puzzled look crossed Darren's face. "What are you doing here, Scarlett?"

Jane rushed to the car. "Can't talk. I'm late."

Darren nodded and walked inside the pizza parlor, turning the placard in the window over to *Open*. Jane was gone before he took his hand from the cardboard sign.

JANE RUSHED THROUGH the aisles at Walmart, looking at the descriptors overhead. It was taking her longer than it should have. She'd lifted a black zip-up hoodie off a rack and was already wearing it over her yellow sweater. She'd picked a size too large, and now the hood was too big for her head—blocking her vision while shopping. Still, she didn't want to drop it. Walmart *did* have cameras but it was busier than a liquor store on payday and Jane sensed she would go unnoticed in the end.

Her list was short: two pillowcases and one

bag of zip ties. She was more comfortable picking out zip ties than linens, so she went to that aisle first.

Hardware was near automotive and for a fleeting moment, Jane felt bad for driving Drunk Sam's car everywhere. She was even sorrier about what she was planning to do to it.

One pack of fourteen-inch, one hundred and twenty-pound cable ties later, she strolled through the linens. She chuckled to herself when she saw the pillowcases with the words *Sweet Dreams* printed on them. She chose black.

Jane couldn't get the image of Three staring her down out of her head. It was the eyes. They were evil. But Jane knew evil. She'd stared it in the face more times than she cared to remember. And it wasn't only because she'd been a Marine.

Three was a monster. He was a monster right in front of her and she was powerless to end him.

She sighed. "Time and place. Right *time*. Right *place*."

Jane chose the self-checkout lane, scanning the barcode on the sleeve of the hoodie first. She paid with cash and kept to herself. The least amount of human contact possible was always her goal. Don't look at anyone, don't ask questions, don't speak.

She was out of the store and back in the car in less than fifteen minutes. With one more stop before going back to Beverly Court to check on Matt, she decided to go through the drive through of a nearby twenty-four-hour burger joint. She felt a little guilty for man-handling Matt earlier and thought if she could bring him food, it might make things a little easier. She'd heard the way to a man's head was through his stomach—or maybe it was his heart. She wasn't sure. What she did know was there was zero food in her apartment, and men were *always* hungry.

Jane ordered burgers and fries and pulled up to pay. She wondered what she was going to say to Matt. She didn't know how to spin what had transpired that morning into something plausible enough for him to believe. He'd asked if she was FBI or CIA. Jane smirked at the thought. *Fat Bald Idiots.* That was what she called the asshats at the FBI. CIA? *Clowns in Action.*

Truth be told, Jane was a little offended at

the thought. She'd rather Matt peg her for a good old fashioned city cop. They were the men and women beating the streets, day in and day out, making less than they should, and putting their lives on the line.

She pulled up and took the food from the woman at the window. "Be safe out there, sugah," the woman drawled. "God bless y'all and have a wonderful day."

Jane looked at her. It was the second time someone had blessed her. She felt compelled to do something she seldom did, reply. "God bless you too."

Jane pulled away from the drive-thru window and checked her mirrors. Even though she was certain Thirteen and Three hadn't followed her, her senses and intuition were on high alert. She opened her backpack while sitting at the red light and took inventory again. She was down one gun, but it didn't matter. Not to Jane. *Always alert. Always prepared.*

Two lights later, Jane neared the Leopard Club. Driving past, she took a chance that Tweedle A and Tweedle B were already giving the dancers their morning hook up. The alley beside the club was vacant, save for a dancer out for a smoke.

She pulled into the gas station on the opposite side of the street, parking at the pump with the Georgia plates facing away from the store. Jane took twenty dollars from the pocket of her bag. Without a credit card, she'd have to go to the window and she'd already scoped eight cameras in the parking lot alone.

Pulling the hoodie up, she crossed her arms as if she was cold, locked the car and hurried to the window outside, covered in bulletproof glass. She stared at her feet as the customer in front of her paid. When it was her turn, she tossed the twenty in the tray and said. "Number three."

She filled up Drunk Sam's car, starting the pump. Then climbing back into the driver's seat, she waited for an automatic shut off at the twenty-dollar mark. She watched the entrance to the strip club intently and measured the distance from the gas station cameras to the back of the alley.

Jane was confident the area where they were dealing smack was out of camera range. Besides, she had a feeling the owner of the upscale strip club had an agreement with the chief of police in town. Somehow the titty bars always did.

The gas line clicked and she jumped from the car to put the nozzle away and get the hell out. On the street in front of her, a dark van slowed to a halt. Using its right turn signal, it waited behind a Jaguar sedan to pull into the parking lot of the strip club. Jane hesitated before getting in the car. She needed a clear view of the plate to positively ID it. Bingo.

Once inside the car, Jane started it with a roar, causing the woman in the minivan next to her to jump. Jane pulled out and immediately crossed traffic, pulling into the parking lot on autopilot and pulled at her backpack.

She'd wrapped the vials of M99 in toilet paper, the Midazolam in notebook paper. The M5050 wasn't wrapped in anything. She felt inside her bag, pulling out the toilet paper clad vial and single syringe tucked into the rubber band that held it all together.

Backing into the alley, she put the car in park, mindful of the distance from the door to the trunk. Jane placed the keys in her front pocket, and removed the safety cap from the syringe.

As much as she wanted to end these two, her direct order was for Thirteen *only*. But that didn't mean she couldn't take Tweedle A and Tweedle B off the streets of Atlanta. That was exactly what she had in mind for the two of them.

She drew up three milligrams of M99; it was a thousand to eighty thousand times more potent than morphine as an analgesic and was used for immobilizing game animals. It caused catatonia at very low dose levels. Its companion M5050 reversed its effects. It was a one to one ratio. Jane was using only one needle. She'd have to be careful not to give one of them a dose that would prove to be unrecoverable. Although if it happened, she wouldn't lose any sleep over it—only her job. Jane flicked the syringe with her finger, working out an air bubble. She knew she couldn't be complacent. Not until she had her shot at Three.

She collected her thoughts and waited for the sole dancer in the alley to make her drug deal and go back inside.

She tucked the syringe in the front pocket of her hoodie and walked to the men with confidence. "My friend, one of the dancers,"

Jane said, pointing to the door. "Told me you had the hook up on some dope."

She stared into the faces of the men. She knew every nuance of Tweedle A's face, down to the scar on his left cheek.

"Are you a cop?" Tweedle B asked.

Jane shook her head and held out two crumpled hundred dollar bills. "Do you want sell it to me or not? I don't have all day."

Tweedle A opened the back of the van and Jane walked forward for a closer inspection of the merchandise. But as she approached, Tweedle B held up his hand. "Stop."

Jane stared at his torso. His clothes were tight, especially his pants. She assumed he was trying to impress the dancers with his maleness, or maybe the lap dances felt better when the pants fit like a glove. Whatever the reason, Jane knew he wasn't packing a weapon. She kept walking.

"Did you hear me, woman?"

Tweedle A pulled his head from the van as Jane took the syringe from her pocket, popping the cap with her thumb.

She got him in the neck before he knew what hit him. B took a step in to throw a punch and Jane delivered a heel to his throat, temporarily stunning his wind pipe. It wasn't much time, but it was enough. Jane took the half used syringe of M99 and injected it into Tweedle B's shoulder. They both dissolved onto the pavement.

Jane stared at their bodies on the ground. "Okay then."

She picked up a scrap piece of rebar lying behind the strip club and slid it through the two door handles on the outside. It would buy her enough time to get their bodies out of the alley. The problem was, they were too heavy to drag all the way to Drunk Sam's car.

In a split-second decision, she picked up the bodies, tossing them into the back of their own van, one at a time. Tweedle A was already halfway there—hanging off the side of the bumper.

She closed the double van doors and took the bar off the back door, walking to the Honda Accord unhurried. *Adapt. Improvise. Overcome.*

Jane unlocked the car, removing her back pack, the Walmart bag and her lunch. Using a Rolling Stones concert t-shirt she found in the back seat, Jane wiped down the inside of the car for fingerprints, pausing only a moment to do the same on the door handle and keychain. She tossed the keys on the driver's side—an open invitation for someone to steal it—then threw the shirt into a nearby dumpster.

Jane climbed aboard the van, pulled the seat up to fit her frame and started it, closing the door. She drove out of the lot, catching the first red light where she eyed the bag of hamburgers.

The light turned green as Jane reached for the brown paper bag and hit the gas. Peeling the paper back, she took a bite and sighed. Drugging terrorists made her hungry.

Next stop, Matt Matthews and Beverly Court.

DAY FIVE | 1200 HOURS

J ANE CLIMBED THE steps two by two to her apartment. One burger and all the fries remained in the grease-stained bag. She was anxious to do something she hadn't done in as long as she could remember—apologize. She liked Matt. She didn't know if she trusted him based on his top-secret file, but she liked him all the same. If she didn't, she wouldn't have cared if he lived or died. Someone pretty high up in the ranks was hiding him. Jane figured in that case, they *couldn't* be upset with her for saving his ass. He was worth something to someone in Washington. Then again, for some reason, if Matt didn't make it, it would be his own damn fault for following Three. No one could get in bed with these people and not suffer the consequences in one way or another.

Jane paused at the top of the stairs. The

sand, already disturbed by their shoes early this morning, was non-existent at the threshold. It meant only one thing. "Sonofabitch."

She shoved the key into the lock and opened the door. On the floor just inside sat his sweaty shirt, shorts and scarf. "Matt?"

Jane walked the small space in thirty seconds. His bag was gone. *He* was gone. She threw the burger bag on the dinette with such force it broke open, fries exploding onto the floor. "*Cocksuckingmotherfuckingsonofabitch!*"

She kung fu kicked her front door shut with her foot, then paused to regroup. Jane hung her hands on her hips and took a deep, cleansing breath. She had a job to do, and keeping Matt Matthews alive wasn't part of it. She'd done all she could to help him. It wasn't going to be enough. She didn't have time to chase after him *and* stop Thirteen's plan. The safety of the many outweighed the safety of one. It was only in that moment that she second-guessed not putting more pressure on him to have sex last night. She'd be forced to go another two or three days—at least until she could get to her next assignment and pick up a random man at a bar. One who could keep his mouth shut, bang her and get the hell out of her life. Matt wasn't about that—not one little bit. "I can't think about this today," she said aloud. "I'll think about it tomorrow."

Jane shook her head, gathered up the burger and fries and tossed them into the kitchen trashcan before walking out the door.

Hustling down the stairs, she opened the back door of the dark van and climbed inside. Taking the zip ties and pillowcases from the shopping bag, it was time to make sure Tweedle A and Tweedle B were adequately restrained should they happen to wake up.

First, she sealed their mouths with duct tape, then cable-tied their feet and hands, linking them together with a third tie. Jane sat back and admired her work. The boys she'd met at the calf roping competition in Texas would be proud.

The final touch was the black hood. It was a favorite used by terrorists, but they didn't have a corner on the market when it came to taking prisoners.

Jane opened the plastic pouch, yanking the two black pillowcases from the packaging. Unceremoniously, she covered their heads, duct taping the material around their necks. It was tight enough to keep it on, but not so tight they couldn't breathe.

She gathered her trash, snapping the needle from the syringe and tossing it out the back of the van. She slipped the rest into a side pocket on her backpack. She'd need to dispose of her evidence before she completed the mission.

Making her way from the back of the vehicle to the front, she climbed over a black leather bag. Finally settled into the driver's seat, she leaned down and unzipped it. "Well, well, well," she said. Jane turned around and looked at the two men she'd bound and taped together. "You boys are going to be *so* disappointed when you wake up."

DAY FIVE | 1230 HOURS

J ANE LOOKED TO her watch. Now half past noon, she'd missed her window to get the job done before lunch. It was a risk, but one she'd have to take. Early morning or late at night was the optimal time to strike. Executing in the middle of the lunch hour rush could be devastating. She prayed her full plan came together. If not, she'd have to adjust. She was forced to play the hand she was dealt.

She drove past the warehouse. The food truck was back, parked at the loading dock. It was hard to know if Thirteen and Three were inside. Driving around the block once, she finally settled on parking one street over. As she climbed out of the van and slung her bag over her shoulders, she could see the back entrance of DeLuca's. The man had expressly asked her not to grace the doors of his business ever again. She wanted to honor his request. But Jane wasn't above lurking behind his place to watch for activity in the building.

She leaned against the outside wall and placed her earbuds in her ears. Hitting play, Mozart's Requiem in D Minor, *Lacrimosa Dies* played in her head and she ticked through every finite detail of how she wanted the elimination to go down. Like an athlete in training, Jane visualized each of her assassinations down to the smallest of detail, putting the energy into the universe in the exact fashion she wanted it to unfold. Manifesting the idea of a successful mission had always translated *into* a successful mission. At least so far. But Jane had never had to deal with a Matt Matthews, and part of her was thankful he'd gone his own way. It was one less thing she had to deal with.

Jane stared at the warehouse. Even though she wasn't getting everything she wanted out of this mission, she knew ending Thirteen got her one step closer to taking out Three. Now that she'd seen the man face to face, she knew everything about him. It was deeper than merely understanding every horrible deed he'd done. More than knowing what his face looked like from photos. Now she'd been near him. She knew his smell, his demeanor, his personality. He would be even easier to eliminate when his number came to her. And Jane was willing to wait. It wasn't her place to choose the targets. Jane wasn't a murderer. If she killed him without a directive, she would be just as evil as he was. The problem now? Three had seen her face too. Sure, she was just a civilian seemingly interested in leasing a rat-infested warehouse, but he knew her all the same. Jane understood that like her, Three would never forget a face. She'd been made, and now she'd would need to change her hair and look. It would be a pain in the ass, but if it helped her get to her ultimate goal, she didn't care.

The powerful chorus sang out with the last *Amen.* The word rang in her head and she began her quiet stroll through the side streets. Four days ago, she was running recon on the building. Today, she would destroy it.

The lunch crowd intensified and DeLuca's Pizza was abuzz with customers. The Greek place beside it was full as well and the delicious smells coming from each of them were attracting even more patrons. Her plan could cause public panic, but for the sake of the thousands who would be taking their children into their workplace in three days, Jane was willing to take that chance.

She walked down the block, deciding it was best to come upon the warehouse from the back door. One block later, she stopped at a dirty payphone booth.

Depositing two quarters, she dialed the number and waited.

"Gary Tinker." He answered the phone like an overzealous dad in a carpool line—glib and cheery.

"Mr. Tinker," Jane said, holding the phone as far away from her ear and mouth as possible without compromising the call. "I'm calling to report a gas leak. It smells like rotten eggs."

"What's your address?"

Jane rattled off the address at the cross streets of the warehouse in Five Points calmly and clearly. There could be no mistakes.

He read the address back to her. "Why didn't you call the emergency li—?"

Jane hung up the phone. Time to move on.

She walked behind the boarded-up dry

cleaning store, taking a dirt path used by the middle school kids to stay off the road. It gave her a clear view of the warehouse as she approached it. She had zero indication as to whether or not Thirteen was home. With two of their group cable-tied in the back of the van, she'd already cut her chances in half of catching one of them off guard. Approaching the side door she'd used over and over, Jane decided to take those odds. Jane would choose death before dishonor.

The door opened easier each time she used it and the usual creak of the rusted metal had worn away, allowing Jane to enter the building silently for the first time.

Without thinking, she placed the cardboard back in the door frame. She wouldn't need it, but Jane believed in a backup for everything. *Two is one and one is none.* If everything went according to plan, Jane would be calmly walking out the front door.

Staying in the back of the building, she exhaled slowly, listening for anything other than her own breath and heartbeat. It was quiet. Jane was pleased.

She moved inside the space and into the

light. The room had changed and was now set up as a chemical work station. Thirteen had been busy during the morning hours. There were bomb vests, a mixing area with a vented makeshift hood. Whoever was making the TATP bombs was now on the premises—and they knew exactly what they were doing.

Jane had to wonder if Three was concocting the bombs himself, or if in his presence, a bomb maker had come to do the job. Jane hadn't exactly prepared for the possibility of a major explosion, leveling the entire area—including DeLuca's businesses across the street.

And then she heard it. A slight murmur from the opposite corner of the building. Jane stepped back into the darkness, but moved closer to the sound. With stealthy skill, she padded her way toward the muffled moan of pain. There was a prisoner on the premises.

A pang of fear rushed through her core. Jane feared Thirteen had taken DeLuca hostage, still angry over the morning's events. She'd heard him distinctly say he wanted to kill the old man. Jane would never forgive herself if anything happened to him. He was a man who'd survived a concentration camp. A cretin like Thirteen didn't deserve to be in DeLuca's presence, let alone be the reason for the end of his life.

Jane leaned into the light for a better look. Behind the makeshift chemistry station and the tables full of plans and propaganda, tied to a chair, bound, hooded, and obviously gagged was Matt Matthews.

Jane dropped her head. *Cocksuckingmotherfuckingsonofabitch.* There he was again, screwing up her plans. *Improvise. Adapt. Overcome.*

Thirteen and Three walked in through the front door. Jane had timed her entrance by the skin of her teeth. But now she had Matt to worry about—again. If she made it out of this assignment alive, she was going to kill Matt Matthews herself.

With a hushed thump, Jane dropped her backpack, taking three things from the bag: a syringe of M99—five milligrams, a second syringe of Midazolam—two milligrams and her gun. Fully loaded, she held it like a best friend—confident in its company. The needles slipped securely into the back pockets of her pants.

"*Make an example of him,*" Three said in

Arabic.

"*It will be my honor to destroy the infidel.*"

"*Do it now.*"

The men hugged and Three was gone.

Jane waited in the background, watching Thirteen as he set up a video camera. As was his norm, the execution would be filmed. Sometimes he did it himself. Sometimes he filmed and praised others. Jane had even watched footage of Thirteen talking a toddler through an execution. The child was prompted to pull the trigger on a semi-automatic weapon. A four-year-old successfully executed a rebel. It was one of the most disturbing things she'd ever seen on tape—and Jane had seen a lot.

"Vy govorite Russian?"

Matt didn't respond. Thirteen kicked his legs, nearly knocking him off the chair. He shouted his question the second time in English. "Do you speak Russian?"

Matt shook his head, *no.* Jane knew his body was sore from beatings by the way he barely moved his neck. It was a *no* all the same.

"Well," he said, drawing out the word. "You're in luck my friend, because the game *we* are going to play—you don't need to *speak*

Russian."

He circled Matt like a predator, striking him on the head at will as he made his way to face the front of his hood before snatching it off. "When you make your way to hell, *writer*, *traitor*, I want you to see where you're going."

Matt squinted in the light, his face swollen from more than just the blows to the head Jane had witnessed.

Thirteen walked to a nearby table and picked up a revolver, making a point to hold it high in the air. He wanted Matt to look at it. "Do you see this?"

Matt remained silent, a bloody gag in his mouth.

"This will be the end of you. But first, let us see how merciful your *god* is."

Thirteen picked up a single bullet from the pile and held it high in the air, examining it carefully. "If your *god* is so powerful, he should protect you from a gun such as this—from a bullet such as this. From a *man* such as me."

Exposing the entire cylinder, he showed Matt the single bullet in his palm before loading it into the chamber and snapping it back into position with a click. Thirteen half-cocked the revolver and spun the chamber, causing a ticking sound. To Jane, it might as well have been nails on a chalkboard.

Thirteen walked toward Matt, grabbing him by the hair to yank his head back, pointing the gun under his exposed chin. "What do you think? Will your *god* save you today, infidel?"

Jane stepped into the light, her gun pointed straight between Thirteen's eyes as she walked fifteen paces, closing the gap between them. "If *He* doesn't, *I* will."

Matt's eyes lit up in relief. His shoulders sank.

Thirteen shook his head, dropping Matt's to fall onto his chest in respite. "I knew you and the old man were planning something. Who are you?"

"Let him go," Jane said, walking closer, not dropping her weapon or the imaginary target she'd painted on his forehead.

"I will kill you both for the camera." Thirteen looked to the heavens and shouted. "This is a blessing!"

Jane shook her head. "It's no blessing. It's the end of the road."

"*What?*" Sarcasm laced his thick accent.

"*You* are going to shoot *me*?"

Jane knew putting a bullet between Thirteen's eyes was a last resort. She suspected he knew that to be true as well. There would be a public outcry. Thirteen's cohorts would retaliate by killing the innocents they could reach—low hanging fruit. She would have to go dark. The government would seek and prosecute her. She would have to leave the country immediately— if she even made it out of the situation alive. Jane walked closer.

"Let him go. This can be between you and me. In fact, take me."

Thirteen let out a deep and resounding belly laugh, showing off his donkey-like features and yellow teeth. "Woman, you are so stupid. How dare you come into my house and tell me what I will and will not do."

Thirteen walked back to Matt. He spun the cylinder again, this time cocking the hammer. He pressed the barrel to Matt's temple. Matt closed his eyes tight, sweat pouring from his rigid body.

Jane had watched vicious murders like this unfold—the victims always closing their eyes— never able to witness their own death. She'd promised herself in the end she would die with her eyes open. She had come into the world helpless, lying in a pile of garbage. She was going out unafraid.

Click

Matt jumped. The first round of Russian roulette was unsuccessful.

Jane walked closer, placing her gun on the ground in front of her. "Okay. You win."

"You are weak. Weak *American*." Thirteen took a step with each accusation. "Kneel, woman!"

Jane knelt, dropping her head to her chest. Placing her hands behind her, she fingered the syringe in her left back pocket—sliding it up into her vise grip.

Thirteen stepped forward, placing the barrel of the gun to the top of Jane's head. Matt moaned across the room. Jane kept her head down. She brought her eyes up to meet Matt's gaze and gave him a wink.

Thirteen rocked on his heels, cocking the revolver once again.

Jane brought her gaze back to the dirty floor of the warehouse, staring at the boots on Thirteen's feet. In one swift motion, she delivered a jarring blow with her left elbow to the inside of his right thigh, racking his testicles. The air left Thirteen's lungs as he gasped at the searing pain. Then, dropping down to bear hug his left calf and ankle, Jane pushed him forward like a defensive lineman holding the goal line. He dropped the gun.

Click

Thirteen landed flat on his back with a horrendous thud. Jane reached across his body, delivering a second blow with her fist to his already injured testicles. Still gripping his thigh, she spun her body in a complete circle on the floor, lifting her leg upon meeting his body again, bringing her heel down to land a third and punishing blow to his manhood. She was already on her feet before his eyes rolled back into his head.

Jane stood fully prepared to kick his ass again—fists up, ready for action. There was none. "Look who's on his knees," she whispered.

Removing the cap from the syringe, she spit it out and walked to him deliberately. She took every step for the women, men and children Thirteen had killed, tortured and abused.

Grabbing him by the hair, she lifted his face to stare into hers, placing her knee in his throat. Her words were direct and calm. "Look at me. I want you to see me. Do you see me?"

Thirteen nodded.

"On your way to hell—to *Jahannam*—I want you to remember this face. You are dying at the hands of a woman. Do you understand? There will be no virgins for you, no beautiful welcome. You are going to burn in *Hellfire* and suffer with Shaitan for the rest of eternity."

Jane's chest heaved with each confident intake of breath. "Tell me you understand what I've just said to you."

Thirteen wept and nodded.

"I can't hear you."

Jane held the lethal dose of M99 to his throbbing jugular vein. His body invited her to end him, but she refused. Not until she heard him say it. Not until he was shamed as he'd shamed so many.

"*Say it!*" she shouted into his face.

"Jahannam." It was a faint whisper. She heard it.

Easing the needle into his neck, Jane delivered the lethal dose with the steady hand of a neurosurgeon. She stood immediately, turning her back on him.

She took a deep breath and walked away, hearing Matt's moans in the background. "I'll be back," she shouted over her shoulder.

Seemingly without a care in the world, Jane walked through the building to the utility closet, straightening her clothes and readjusting the tension in her ponytail. She opened the door and lay on the floor, wiggling her body to gain access to the single hot water heater that served the two bathrooms.

Blowing out the pilot light on the old heater, she spied the gas line clearly marked with an orange inspection tag. Picking up the hammer she'd planted, she gave the pipe two swift blows. She didn't want to open it completely, but aimed for a significant leak.

The smell of rotten eggs overcame her at once. She'd hit too hard. Her careful plan had turned into a game of beat the clock.

DAY FIVE | 1330 HOURS

IMPROVISE. ADAPT. OVERCOME.

Walking to Matt, she flipped open the switchblade she kept in her boot and released the ties cutting into his wrists. Next his feet.

Matt rubbed his skin for only a moment before pulling the gag from his bloody and swollen mouth. "Who the hell *are* you?"

Jane spoke but didn't look him in the face. "I think the phrase you're looking for is, *thank you for saving my sorry ass. I should've listened to you in the first place and stayed at your apartment.*"

"Scarlett," he said grabbing her by the hand.

Jane rolled her eyes. "Not now."

She motioned for him to follow her. Jane wanted her guns—the one Thirteen kicked across the floor and the one taped behind the filing cabinet. There wasn't time. Instead she took the revolver with one bullet from the dead hand of Thirteen, sweeping it up in her palm and tucking it in the back of her pants. She thought nothing of stepping over his lifeless body. Matt couldn't stop looking at it and tripped over Thirteen's boots while walking away. "Stop messing around," Jane said. "We've got to go."

"Is that gas I smell?" he asked, making a face.

Jane opened the back door, looking both ways before taking Matt's hand and slipping out into the fresh air. "Follow me," Jane said, leading him away from the warehouse.

Outside fire engines and police cars blocked the streets—lights were flashing and were people rushing away from the scene.

"What's going on?" Matt asked, squinting in the sunshine.

"Just follow me." Jane didn't look back. The assignment wasn't complete. She needed to get Matt to safety. Following the dirt path behind the buildings, Jane took him to a nearby tree and sat him down. "Rest here," she said. "None of this happened. You don't know me. If you want to stay alive, you can't remember anything."

"Wait."

Before Matt could utter another word, Jane stuck the remaining needle from her pocket into his exposed arm—two milligrams of Midazolam coursed through his bloodstream. In less than twenty seconds, Matt Matthews was asleep. Jane walked away and across the street. She didn't look back. She never looked back.

Rushing to the sweet spot she'd chosen, Jane hurried past all the police and firemen, pretending to be a regular citizen getting out of harm's way as best she could.

She looked to her watch. Time was slipping away and now that she carried Thirteen's gun loaded with one bullet, she had one chance. Jane had one shot.

Finding a place on the grassy knoll, Jane opened the chamber of the revolver, lining the one bullet to fire correctly. She lay down on the ground, and took aim at the shining can of acetone high in the blacked out window of the warehouse.

Taking a deep breath, she cocked the hammer, thankful for a calm day with no wind. She was thirty yards from her target. If she missed, her mission would be a failure.

She closed one eye, and took dead aim.

"Who are you?"

Jane recognized the voice and a chill ran through her body. She came to her feet, her backpack sliding off her shoulder and onto the ground as she stared him in the face. Standing in her way. Standing in her direct line of fire. Three.

Jane felt the damp perspiration chill on her forehead as a gentle breeze kicked up. Wet with a constant flow of natural epinephrine coursing through her body, her hands remained steady. Jane choked the gun but caressed the trigger with her finger. The hair on her arms lifted in anticipation. Standing in his presence, Jane found herself in a far-away place—a dream— part of a mirage. Together they stood face to face, as if they were the only two people who existed. The rest of the world faded into a background of muffled whispers.

Jane stared into his smug expression. Her skin crawled. She answered. "I'm no one."

He took a step toward her and Jane lifted the .357 Magnum. Pointing it at his head, she was rooted to her spot. "Don't come any closer."

The hate-fire of revenge filled Jane's dark soul. She glanced only once to the shining can sitting in the window—waiting for her to finish what she'd begun.

"Who are you?" He asked the question again. Three's calm nature only fueled her need to end him.

Jane had one bullet. Jane had one choice.

Three stepped toward her. Jane took aim, exhaled and squeezed off the only round in the chamber. The kick from the gun was powerful and Jane took a step back as the bullet whizzed through the air to its target.

It was a delay of two seconds or more and it was over. Old man DeLuca's warehouse exploded in a white-hot flash of fire, natural gas and chemicals. Jane was blown off her feet, her ears ringing. She rolled over and stared into the black smoke. Debris rained down from the sky. Ten feet away from her was Three, face down on the grass, his arms and legs moving. Bloody cuts covering him, none of them deep, he was still alive.

She pulled herself from the ground, picked up the gun and her backpack. The block looked like a warzone. Parts of the warehouse were everywhere, most of the building itself gone. Somehow the storefront of DeLuca's wasn't damaged, save for the sign which now hung on by a thread to the front of his building. The same couldn't be said for the Greek sandwich shop. It would need serious rehab.

Slinging her backpack over her shoulder, Jane gave Three a fleeting glance, then stopped. They locked eyes for a mere moment. Jane turned. Another day. Another time. Thirteen was dead. Her mission was complete. She didn't look back. She never looked back.

DAY FIVE | 1430 HOURS

MAKING HER WAY through the crowd of police and firemen, she pointed to the black van parked one street behind DeLuca's. "Officer, I just want to get my van out of here," she said pointing with her key.

He waved her through, giving her specific instructions on which route to take for evacuation. She agreed and hurried to the vehicle.

Jane unlocked the passenger door, taking the black leather bag shoved between the bucket seats by the top handles. She took two stacks out before zipping it up again, then slung it over her shoulder and closed the door. It was heavier than she'd expected.

Dodging the watchful eye of the police officers in the area, she walked to the back door of DeLuca's, letting herself in. The kitchen was empty, but Jane could hear voices in the main area of the restaurant.

Opening a cold pizza oven, Jane shoved the black leather bag inside, shutting the door. It would be days, maybe weeks before the gas ovens would be ready to fire again.

Ordering pads and pens sat in the corner by the clean aprons. Jane took one to leave parting words for DeLuca.

Thank you again for breakfast this morning. I didn't have any money with me at the time, but I came back to leave you a tip. It's in the oven. Be well.

"Scarlett?"

Jane looked up from her note to find DeLuca standing in the doorway.

"Scarlett, are you okay?"

It was only then Jane caught her reflection in the shining stainless steel of the kitchen table. She was black—covered in debris and soot. A tiny cut on her forehead was bleeding. Jane was oblivious to all of it. "I'm fine."

"What are you doing here?"

"I wanted to—I wanted to thank you—for breakfast this morning."

DeLuca cocked his head in confusion.

"Yes. Thank you." Jane pointed to him and

gave him a rare smile. She opened the back door to leave and stopped, wadding the paper note she'd written in her hand. Pointing to the oven Jane looked to her feet. She felt bad for the explosion—for the time it would take for his family to recover—it showed on her face. "I ah…I left you a little something in the oven. Just a little thank you for…like I said…. breakfast."

DeLuca nodded, but didn't say anything.

Jane walked away, shutting the door behind her. She had one more stop.

INSIDE HIS PIZZERIA kitchen, eighty-three-year-old Marco DeLuca opened the oven and found a black leather bag. He looked around the room as if someone might be watching, then pulled it out, placing it on the counter in the center of the kitchen.

Unzipping it, stacks of new one hundred dollar bills wrapped in mustard paper bands that read, *$10,000* spilled onto the counter. He counted as many as he could. When he reached seven hundred thousand, he zipped up the bag.

He looked around the room once again, then hurried to the back door to look for her. She was already gone.

DAY FIVE | 1445 HOURS

JANE DROVE THE van out of the Five Points area, staying just on the outside of the police perimeter. The last part of her plan was to wake Tweedle A and Tweedle B up from their catatonic nap and leave them where they could be found inside a van filled with heroin and cash. She chose a spot the police would sweep that wasn't visible to a camera, and parked.

Jane climbed through the van, stepping over the bodies as she took her backpack from her shoulders. Taking one syringe, she filled it with M5050, the antidote to the animal tranquilizer she'd used. Giving them an equal amount from the same syringe, she recapped it and slipped it into her dirty jacket pocket. Climbing out the back, she closed the van doors just as the boys were waking up.

Jane straightened the jacket across her shoulders and wiped the sweat from her brow. Twenty yards from the van, she knew they were awake when one of them began kicking the door from the inside. It wouldn't be long now.

She was still a good mile from Beverly Court, and it was time to walk that way. Pulling the small plastic bottle of hand sanitizer from the side pocket of her bag, she squirted the last of it into her palms and began to rub. She needed a shower, an internet connection, and a place to dump her trash.

Now that she'd met Three face to face, there was nothing that could stop her from taking the man down—that was—when his number finally came up. And it would. Jane knew it would.

She wondered if Matt had made it to the hospital okay. She thought about going to check on him, but hospitals were tight—their surveillance was good and it wouldn't be worth it. She'd saved his life. It seemed like that should've been enough.

When Jane finally made it to the parking lot of Beverly Court, she looked up, shielding the sun from her face, to see a package sitting at her front door. Her new assignment had arrived.

She climbed the steps two by two—a little slower than usual. Jane picked up the package and stuck it under her arm to dig out her keys.

"You doin' okay sweetie?"

Melly was out of her apartment again in her nightgown and two sets of glasses. Why she wore two, Jane would never have the pleasure of discovering. "I'm fine, thank you."

Melanie Munroe smiled and waved her off before closing her door.

Jane let herself in, dropping her bag at her feet and locking the door behind her. She stumbled to the bathroom and turned on the water. There on the floor was a pair of black compression shorts—Matt's shorts. Jane imagined him taking off his clothes as she unbuttoned her pants and pulled the sullied yellow sweater over her head.

Naked, she climbed over the side of the tub, allowing the water to wash over her. As the soap and shampoo cleansed her body, Jane longed for her mind to be rinsed clean too. All she'd thought about for the last four years was ending Three. Now she second guessed every aspect of her day, deconstructing it point by point.

She couldn't go back. She could only move forward. She'd stared evil in the face and knew in her heart it wasn't a matter of *if*, but *when* they would meet again.

DAY SIX | 1200 HOURS

I T HAD BEEN a productive day, and it was only noon. Taking the bus to the library, Jane logged into her social media account and posted on her wall. It was a shared post from a mommy blog entitled, *Thirteen ways to be successful in the office and at home.* It was her way of letting Crow know her mission had been accomplished, although Jane suspected that since the kill had gone off with a bang instead of a whimper, Crow already knew. Still, it was protocol for her to check in.

She logged out and said goodbye to the staff, telling them she'd be back in to volunteer tomorrow afternoon. But Jane would never be back. She took the bus to her apartment, stopping at the payphone on the corner to make a single call. She used the prepaid long distance card she'd purchased at the gas station in Texas and dialed the phone. When he answered, a sense of calm in the aftermath of the storm filled her.

"Father Doheny?"

"Yes. Who is this?"

"Father, it's me."

There was a moment of silence. She wouldn't say her name. She *couldn't* say her name. Father Doheny knew who she was all the same.

"How are you?"

"I'm fine. I mean, I guess I'm fine. Tired. Sometimes I feel the weight of the world on my shoulders."

"Burdens are for shoulders strong enough to carry them."

"I don't know if I'm that person, Father. I think I'm just doing the best I can. I *am* getting closer to finishing up what I started."

"I guess *that's* a good thing."

"It is."

"I keep you in my prayers."

"I guess *that's* a good thing," Jane said, repeating his words.

"When are you coming to visit me? You know I'll be retiring soon."

Jane took a beat. "When?"

"I haven't set a date, but I wanted you to know. It would be wonderful if you came into town to celebrate it with me."

"Sure." Jane knew the possibility of this happening was zero. She would need to make an unannounced visit to Pittsburgh to retrieve her things from his safe before Father Doheny set sail into the sunset of a clergy retirement home.

"Are you sure you're okay?" he asked.

"I just wanted to hear a friendly voice."

"You know you don't have to wait until I retire. You're always welcome here, my child."

"Thank you, Father. I need to run."

"You're always on the run, aren't you?"

"I'm hoping to slow down soon."

"Good. When you do, come visit me."

"I'll do my best."

"Take care."

"You too, Father."

Jane hung up. After speaking with Father Doheny, she usually felt better about her life and her work, but today she just felt empty. This mission had really taken the wind from her sails. It was a million-dollar job and she was thankful for the money. Each deposit was one step closer to the end.

Walking back to her apartment, she ticked through her inventory list. She'd disposed of every article of clothing and all toiletries she wasn't taking with her, and packed her backpack with only the essentials. Jane had emptied the medicine cabinet into her bag, taking her pharmacy with her to the next mission. She also had the memorized images of the information in Matt's closet in her mind.

Opening the door, she sat in the plaid chair, staring at the book that gave her the destination and target of her next assignment. She'd wiped the apartment down with Clorox, leaving no trace of her time there. Except for the sheets on her bed, she was ready to go. Jane contemplated staying one more night in Atlanta. She told herself it was to catch up on her sleep. But that was a lie and she knew it.

The bus station was within walking distance and she'd already memorized the schedule for tonight and tomorrow. Walking to the bathroom, she took a look at herself in the mirror. Her long brown hair would have to go. She'd need to change her looks up regularly now that she'd been made by Three. It was a detail she'd left out of her cryptic post online for Crow.

She stared into the reflection of her blue eyes, letting her imagination drift into the future, where she lived a normal life as a student in Stockholm. After speaking with Father Doheny, she knew her time to end Three was limited. Whether she wanted to retire or not, it was going to happen.

A knock came at her door. She flinched and immediately cursed herself for not taking the first bus out of town that morning.

She peered between the curtain and the window. She had two choices. She could open the door, or pretend she was already gone.

"C'mon Scarlett. I know you're in there. Your neighbor Melly told me you just got back home. Open up. I need to see you."

His face bruised, his left eye, black and swollen, Matt had two butterfly strips across a deep cut on his forehead.

For the first time since Jane set foot in Atlanta to eliminate Thirteen, she felt a pang of fear. What would she tell him? It wouldn't be the truth. What would she ask of him? She wouldn't believe his answer.

Jane watched Matt place his open palm on the door, leaning his head in to rest. He mumbled the word only to himself. "Please."

She opened the door and stood back, silently inviting him to enter, then shut the door behind him and took two steps away, crossing her arms.

"Scar—"

Jane put her hand in the air. She didn't want to hear him say that name. Not anymore.

They stared at one another. Matt's eyes glazed over with tears. Jane acknowledged his emotion and gave him the tiniest of nods, but didn't say a word.

"I don't know—"

Jane put her hand in the air a second time. "Don't."

"But I—"

"Matt?" Jane tilted her head and raised an eyebrow.

He smiled, and for a moment looked away, hanging his hands on his hips. "Yes?"

"Don't talk."

Matt tucked his lips inside his mouth and gave her an exaggerated nod. "Fine. No talking."

"Matt?"

"Yes?"

"You're still talking."

Matt swallowed hard and walked across the small apartment to Jane without dropping his gaze. He placed his hands on her shoulders, gripping her small but powerful frame in his bruised hands. He studied her face. She let him, not turning away from his loving stare.

Matt pulled her close and brushed his lips against the smoothness of her skin, kissing her cheek and holding it for longer than necessary. Moving up her face to lightly caress her closed eyes with his swollen lips, he gave each a lingering kiss. He pulled away, looking deep into her eyes. Jane dropped her head back, inviting him into her mouth.

The kiss was sweetness—a drugging nectar. It wasn't the usual hard lipped, deep throat tongue hockey she'd worked her way past in other sexcapades just to get to the payoff— Matt's kiss was tender and caring, and Jane drank it in before she had a moment to think better of it.

His arms surrounded her, hard and confident. Jane, a woman so sure of herself in the world of terror, became helpless at the rush of emotion—the sinking and yielding tide of warmth that filled her body and left her weak.

Jane clung to him, his insistent mouth caressing her lips sent a wave of tremors through her core, awakening sensations Jane had never known she was capable of experiencing.

She gasped between the passionate kisses that were bringing her to her knees. "Matt."

Picking her up off the ground, he carried her to the bedroom and carefully laid her body across the bed, climbing on top of her. He kissed his way down her neck with care, peeling back her shirt to run his tongue across her delicate collarbone.

"Matt."

He kissed his way across her chest and paused to look at her. "Don't talk."

Jane gave in to the new feeling, the dizzy giddiness she felt circled round and round in her head, and in that moment she realized she wasn't being kissed—she was kissing him back.

DAY SEVEN | ZERO DARK THIRTY

MATT LAY ON his back, completely naked. Jane threw her leg across the bruised and bare contours of his torso. He rested his open palm on her tight and muscular bottom. A thin layer of glistening satisfaction covered their bodies. Jane could feel his heart beat—the pulse strong against the hand she splayed across his chest. Their bodies were damp with exhaustion and afterglow.

The sex had been exceptional. There were no inhibitions or mishandlings of the other's needs. It was as if they were made for one another. The second time was even better. The third a mind-blowing experience Matt said he was certain no two creatures on earth had ever experienced outside the tiny room at Beverly

Court.

Jane shifted her weight, curling into the nook of his arm. He laced his fingers with hers and let out a satisfied sigh. They were spent.

Jane ran her fingers across the bruised cuts around his wrists—evidence of the past two days. He'd not asked. She'd not offered. Slowly he drifted into the kind of sleep only experienced by lovers. Sated. Secure.

Jane waited until she was certain Matt was in a deep slumber before rolling out of the bed without making a sound. She dressed silently, finding her clothes around the room, and gathered her belongings—her backpack, now full of everything she wanted or needed to take with her. Everything except Matt.

She took a moment and stood in the doorway of the bedroom. She didn't want to walk away—not yet. The moonlight shone through a crack in the curtains, lighting his face. Jane thought he looked like an angel—so peaceful, so full of love and hope—and for the first time in her adult life she had a *what if* moment.

It was fleeting.

Jane dropped her head, reminding herself who she really was and walked out of the bedroom to don her full backpack. She pulled her newest book from the side pocket and tucked it under her arm. Quietly opening the door, Jane stepped into the moonlight and turned to leave. Lying on the floor atop Matt's t-shirt and running shorts was his shemagh—his scarf.

Jane picked it up and held it to her face. It smelled of Matt. The feeling was beyond her in that moment and she wrapped it around her neck, breathing him in. She shut the door to her apartment at Beverly Court and walked away. She didn't look back. Jane never looked back.

DAY SEVEN | 0700 HOURS

MATT ROLLED OVER. The bed was cold. She was gone. He rubbed the sleep from his eyes and sat on the edge. The door to the bathroom was closed. He stood and knocked twice. When no one answered, he opened it. The apartment was empty.

He surveyed the floor, finding his boxers, jeans and t-shirt. He got dressed and walked into the other room. There was no note. There was no Scarlett.

Sitting on the side of the bed, he decided he could fool himself into believing she was coming back—but he'd only sit in her apartment all day waiting. He knew in his heart she was gone.

Matt found his shoes and his field coat, taking them both into the little den of her apartment. Slipping on his loafers, he dug his arms into the coat and noticed his running clothes still in a pile by the door where he'd left them. It seemed like a lifetime ago, and yet it was only two days. He picked them up and opened the front door, turning only to say a silent goodbye to the best night of his life.

He shut the door and lay his open palm against the numbers. "I'll never forget you."

Matt looked over the railing of the third floor and spied his BMW. When he turned back, Scarlett's neighbor Melly stood in front of him. She wore two pairs of glasses on her face and the kind of housecoat Matt hadn't seen since his great-grandmother was alive.

Melly Munroe pointed to Jane's apartment. "She's gone."

Matt nodded.

"She's gone," she repeated.

"I know. The question is, where?"

The old woman pointed to Jane's apartment emphatically. "She's fallen down a rabbit hole, that one."

"Rabbit hole?"

Melly nodded slowly. Deliberately. "There's no use going back to yesterday, because she was a different person then."

Matt shook his head. The old woman wasn't making any sense, but she didn't look like the kind of person who was supposed to. "What are you trying to say?"

"Never mind young man." Melly waved him off. "We're all mad here."

Matt narrowed his gaze and watched the woman sashay back into her apartment. He gave the door a fleeting glance, then took the stairs one by one, all the way to the bottom floor.

He climbed into his car and turned the ignition. He didn't know where he was going next, or what was going to do. The sound of his phone ringing startled him and he searched the pockets of his coat, finally retrieving it.

"Matthews," he said.

At first the line was silent except for heavy breathing. Then a voice spoke softly. "Do you still want to meet?"

Matt turned off the car. "Who is this?"

"The Instructor."

Matt was beyond stunned and consequently remained silent.

The heavy breathing commenced again, then finally, "Hello?"

"Yes. I'm still here."

"Do you?"

Matt didn't hesitate. "Yes."

"I have some conditions."

Matt pulled a reporter's notebook from the glove compartment and a pen from his visor. "I'm listening."

DAY FORTY-THREE | 0800 HOURS

S AM GOODWIN WALKED into the library with newfound energy. It was his first day back at the library after an extended vacation that afforded him the opportunity to get his life together and start divorce proceedings. He hadn't had a drop of alcohol in forty-two days and he was feeling pretty damn good about it.

He glad-handed with the ladies out front who'd missed him terribly, and he doted on Stella, who'd taken over his duties while he was away. Everyone remarked on how rested he looked. They chatted about the recent explosion near the library and Sam explained how the police had found his car in an abandoned parking lot. The Honda Accord had been stripped of everything and his insurance company had made good on it. Sam Goodwin had a new life, a new love and a new car.

He walked into his office. He'd not stepped foot in it since the day he left. Sitting in his chair, he opened the bottom drawer—the place he'd always hidden his booze, and prayed Scarlett had the forethought to throw it all away.

Sam let out a sigh of relief. There was no alcohol, only a manila envelope with his name written across the top.

Running his thumb under the seal, he opened it, dropping the contents onto his desktop. Sam's jaw dropped and he sat back in his chair. A bundle of hundred dollar bills was wrapped in a mustard gold, ten-thousand-dollar currency strap. Five one hundred dollar bills were paper-clipped together with a piece of paper folded three times.

Dear Sam,

I hope this note finds you well. I'm afraid I can no longer volunteer at the Drake Library, but I wanted to leave you with a small token of my appreciation. Please use this money to start a program for children in this area— specifically foster kids. They are prisoners to other people's problems. It would be nice if they had an opportunity to escape them. As Margaret Mitchell once wrote in Gone With the

Wind, "hardships make or break people." My wish is that these children have a fighting chance to break out of their hardships. I know I can count on you to help.

P.S. The five hundred is for you. Start your life with Albert or whomever. Keep holding it together Sam, and don't look back. I never do.

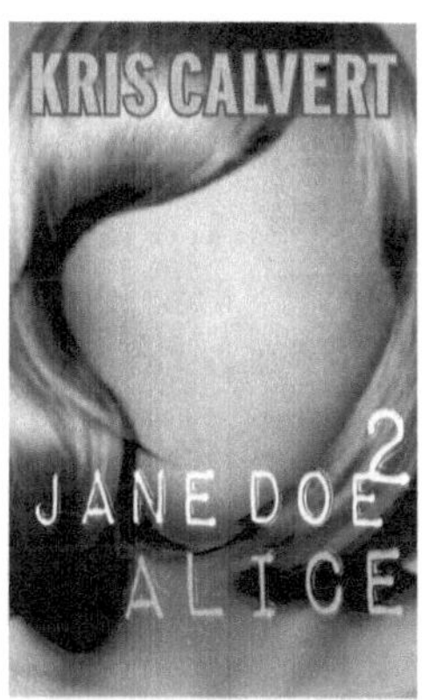

Jane Doe 2 – Alice

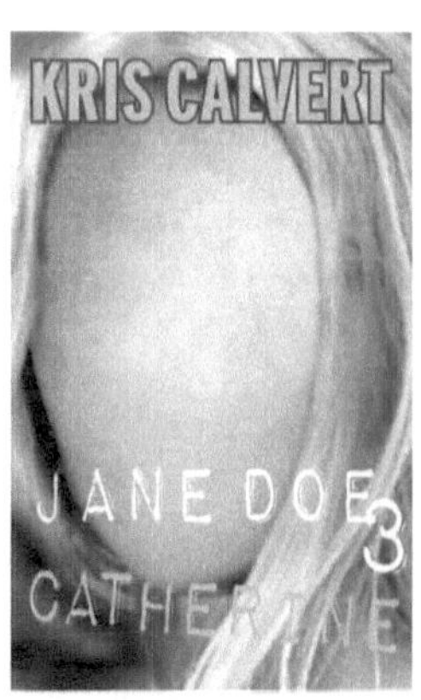

Jane Doe 3 – Catherine

Kris Calvert is a former copywriter and PR mercenary who after some coaxing, began writing novels. She loves alliteration, pearls and post-it notes. She's married to the man of her dreams and lives in Lexington, Kentucky. She's Momma to two grown children and is also responsible for one very needy dog. When she's not writing, she's baking cupcakes.

WEBSITE: www.kriscalvert.com

EMAIL: info@kriscalvert.com

TWITTER: @kriscalvert

FACEBOOK:
www.facebook.com/kriscalvert30

BLOG: www.calvertwrites.blogspot.com

NEWSLETTER
www.kriscalvert.com/Kris_Calvert/NEWSLE
TTER.html

www.ingramcontent.com/pod-product-compliance
Lightning Source LLC
Chambersburg PA
CBHW051639180726
48284CB00006B/1798